SHADOW THE BARON

SHADOW THE BARON

John Creasey
as
Anthony Morton

Curley Publishing, Inc.
South Yarmouth, Ma.

Library of Congress Cataloging-in-Publication Data

Creasey, John.
　Shadow the baron / John Creasey as Anthony Morton.—Large print ed.
　　p. cm.
　1. Large type books.　I. Title.
[PR6005.R517S49　1991]
823'.912—dc20
ISBN 0–7927–0715–X

91-12337
CIP

© **John Creasey 1951**

All rights reserved. No part of this book may be used or reproduced in any manner without written permission except in the case of brief quotations embodied in critical articles and reviews.

Published in Large Print by arrangement with the author's estate.

Printed in Great Britain

SHADOW THE BARON

John Creasey as Anthony Morton

Superintendent Bristow of New Scotland Yard was worried, worried enough to ask John Mannering – alias The Baron – to help him catch The Shadow, a mysterious jewel thief. This elusive thief, with a dozen robberies to his credit, had left no trace as to his identity. And Mannering, determined to track down the criminal, finds that the pursuer becomes the pursued...

CHAPTER ONE

THE DETECTIVE TAKES A WALK

Superintendent Bristow, of New Scotland Yard, had always believed that he could think best when walking. During cold January and bleak February, he had walked a great deal. That had helped to keep him warm. At the end of the two months, he doubted the efficacy of walking as an aid to constructive thinking. Yet he persisted.

On the first day of March, Spring came to London. The sun spread a kindly warmth over the throngs in the West End. The daffodils on the barrows and in the baskets of the Piccadilly flower sellers cried heavily that winter had gone. Dark thoughts, however, haunted Bristow, a tall, spruce, well-dressed man, blind to all but the hoarse insistence of a newsboy.

"Nother big jewel robbery—speshul!"

Bristow reached the Circus, and waited with a small crowd for the traffic to pause. A little man, poorly dressed, unshaven but bright-eyed, caught sight of him, and his eyes grew sharper.

The traffic lights shone green.

Bristow moved across the road towards Eros. The little man followed. One of the flower sellers, a massive woman bundled up in overcoats, with an incongruous feathered hat perched on masses of dusty hair, waved a plump hand to him.

'''Allo, ducks,' she greeted. 'Nice die.'

'Beautiful,' said Bristow, mechanically. 'Trade any better, Lil?'

'Best mornin' I've 'ad this year,' said Lil. She did not need to ask what Bristow wanted, but from a small tray she took a single gardenia. With this in her hand, she lumbered up, breathing with gusty energy. She placed the gardenia in Bristow's button-hole, fastening it into position. Bristow gave her his daily shilling.

'Beauty, that one is an' no mistake,' said Lil. 'Saved it for you, Mr. Bristow. *You* busy?'

'I need a holiday,' declared Bristow.

Lil chuckled comfortably. 'Don't you worry, ducks. You'll get 'im. Up to 'is tricks again last night, wasn't 'e?'

'You bet he was,' said the little man, who stood close by. '''Morning, Super!'

Bristow looked at him without favour.

'Know anything about him, Clip?'

'Who, me? Not my cup of tea, Super.' The little man spoke in a pseudo cultured voice from a mouth widened in a mechanical grin.

'Besides, I'm an honest member of the British public now, didn't anyone tell you?'

'They must have forgotten,' said Bristow. 'Goodbye, Lil.'

'Bye bye, dearie!'

Bristow moved round the statue and crossed towards Shaftesbury Avenue, and now the little man walked with him.

Another newsboy shrilled:

'Big jewel robbery, read all abaht it!'

'What, not going to buy a paper?' asked his self-appointed companion, flashing coppers from his pocket, as he took an *Evening News*. 'Accept it from me, with my compliments.'

Bristow took the paper.

'Chirpy this morning, aren't you?'

The little man chuckled.

'Always does me good when I see you wearing a frown, Super! Not that I mean any malice, mind you, but this chap keeps you on your toes, doesn't he? How much stuff has he lifted? Can't be far short of a hundred thousand quid, can it? Been busy six months, done a dozen jobs and shown you a clean pair of heels every time. You've got to hand it to him.'

'That's right,' said Bristow. 'I'll hand him a pair of handcuffs one of these days.'

'Not if you live to be a thousand.' The little man rubbed his hands together with slow enjoyment. 'He's made a fool of you and everyone at the Yard, Super. Good luck to him, I say. So long.' With an airy wave of the hand he slipped into a door of Lyons Corner House.

Bristow crossed to Leicester Square, where every seat was filled with basking people, and opened the newspaper. He read stoically:

£15,000 GEMS STOLEN FROM WEST END FLAT
'SHADOW' STRIKES AGAIN

Daring jewel-thief, known as 'The Shadow' broke into the Mayfair flat of Mr. Raymond Allen during the night and in spite of the most up-to-date burglar alarm escaped with beautiful Mrs. Allen's jewels. The loss is estimated at £15,000. No one was disturbed although four people were sleeping on the premises.

The theft appears to have been the work of the man known as 'The Shadow' and is the tenth of a series of burglaries attributed to him.

Superintendent William Bristow, the Yard's jewel expert, was at the flat early this morning. The Yard has no statement to make.

Bristow tucked the paper under his arm, and became aware of the slightly malicious grin of a stationary taxi-driver.

Bristow paused.

'Happy?' he inquired.

'Happier than you are, I shouldn't wonder.'

'Hope he'll get off?'

'Oh, I wouldn't go as far as that,' said the cabby. 'Can't help but admire him though, can you? I must say you don't look as if you've been up all night, Mr. Bristow.'

'I haven't,' said Bristow curtly.

At Trafalgar Square, a car slid past him in purring luxury; a Sunbeam Talbot, driven by a middle-aged man smoking a cigar. The car reminded Bristow of another man who owned a Sunbeam Talbot, a man who was probably as sympathetic as the cabby to 'The Shadow's' evasion of arrest.

Bristow reached a tobacconist's near the Yard, and within sight of the Cenotaph and Parliament Square, and he went in. The woman who managed the shop was sitting, head bent, over a newspaper. She jumped up.

'If it isn't Mr. Bristow!'

'Why the surprise? I look in most days.'

'Just reading about you,' she said, 'you must be having a very worrying time, Mr. Bristow. Forty *Players* as usual?' She dipped under the counter. 'But I must say, he's a proper spark, isn't he? You've got to admire him—how anyone *dare* do what he does, I just don't know. Isn't it the day to fill your lighter?'

'Thanks.' Bristow handed over his lighter. 'If he breaks into your house tonight and takes everything of value, will you still admire him?'

She laughed. 'Well, if you put it that way, I wouldn't, not that *I've* got anything worth pinching. Only goes for the rich, doesn't he? There's no need for me to worry. There you are—last you the rest of the week.'

'Thanks,' said Bristow, and turned towards the Yard, along the narrow street which led from Parliament Street. The policemen on duty touched their foreheads, and Bristow grunted. He walked through the Civil Duties building and the newer C.I.D. to his office. His chief *aide*, Chief Inspector Gordon, was sitting at one of the desks.

''Morning, Bill.'

''Morning, Pat.'

'A-K wants a word with you.'

'I'm not surprised. Anything in?'

'Just got the report from the Allens' place, but there's not a clue.'

Bristow grunted, and went out again.

Colonel Anderson-Kerr, the Assistant Commissioner at the Yard, was to be found in his own larger office on the next floor. He was a small, leathery-looking whippet of a man, with piercing blue eyes. Meticulously tidy, his desk supported in geometical order, two telephones, an inkstand, a box of cigarettes, an ashtray, and a single file of papers. Many at the Yard disliked him, most were apprehensive in his presence. Bristow, however, both liked and respected the man.

Anderson-Kerr motioned to a chair.

'What time did you get to Bingham Court?'

'The safe was opened in the same way as all the others. There could be two or three men with the same trick, but it's not likely.'

Anderson-Kerr's eyebrows shot up.

'Meaning, you think it might be a team?'

'I have wondered.'

'Well, I hope not,' said Anderson-Kerr, and pushed the cigarettes across the desk. 'You know, Bristow, we're going to have a bad time. This chap's getting a lot of sympathy. He'll get more, until he makes a fool of himself and hurts someone. Why the devil do people have a soft spot for a man like this? It's happened time and time again.' He moved irritably. 'You say there isn't a line of any kind—no squeal, nothing at the receivers' places?'

'Nothing.'

'Any idea what he does with the stuff?'

'Either he's keeping it in cold storage until the heat's switched off, or he's sending it abroad. I think it goes abroad—there aren't many of his sort who can afford to wait months before they turn the stuff into money. I'm having a special check at the Channel ports and all airports. If we find that someone who left the country after one of the other jobs, goes this time, we can hold him for questioning. We might find the stuff on him, too.'

'But you don't think so.'

'I'm almost past thinking,' said Bristow. 'Except crazy ideas.' He smiled faintly.

'How crazy?'

'Completely.'

'I see,' said Anderson-Kerr. He rose decisively, and moved to the window. 'Set a thief to catch a thief?' he suggested.

Bristow said: 'So it's been in your mind, too?'

'I keep turning it out. The Shadow is beginning to win as big a reputation as that enjoyed by the Baron in the bad old days. The Baron used the same methods, barred violence, had the same uncanny knack of getting in and out of places without being seen, and could do what he liked with any safe he tackled. They must use the same wand! Now if the Baron went after the Shadow—' He broke off.

'There's a difference.'

'What is it?'

'After the third job, I knew the Baron was John Mannering. After ten jobs, I don't know the Shadow. That makes the Shadow the better man—so far.'

'Hmm.' Anderson-Kerr swung round. 'Oh, forget it. It's impossible. We can't use Mannering.'

Bristow half closed his eyes.

'I knew Mannering as the Baron, and he got away with it. The vital little bit of evidence was always missing. He's played the fool in a thousand ways since the Baron days, but he's no longer a thief. Whether he'd work against the Shadow on the present score, I don't know. He would, if a murder were committed, but—' Bristow shrugged.

'We're both getting soft in the head,' growled Anderson-Kerr. 'We can't use him.'

'We couldn't approach him ourselves on this kind of job,' Bristow agreed. 'But we might fix something. One of the Shadow's earlier victims was Toby Plender. Plender and Mannering used to be fairly intimate. Now if Plender asked Mannering—' Bristow broke off, rubbing his chin. 'We could rely on Plender. He's a first-class lawyer and a very good friend. If I dropped a hint to him, he might make a personal appeal to Mannering, and Mannering would probably jump to it. Like me to try?'

'I see no cause why we shouldn't do that,' said Anderson-Kerr slowly, 'except that Mannering would probably guess the reason, if Plender suggests it now—the Plender job is, after all, four months old.'

Bristow smiled; he looked more cheerful than when he had walked across Leicester Square.

'It doesn't matter what Mannering guesses, and he probably has a pretty good idea what we're feeling, already. Shall I see Plender?'

'Go ahead,' said Anderson-Kerr.

Bristow hummed to himself as he walked along the passages, and beamed at Gordon as he sat down at his desk. The sound of the traffic on the Embankment was loud this morning, for the window was open. Ponderously, fatefully, Big Ben chimed the hour.

'Caught the Shadow?' inquired Gordon.

Bristow laughed.

'We've decided on a different bait.'

'Ah. No one can say you've rushed things,' Gordon said sardonically.

He cogitated the advisability of saying more, decided on its unwisdom, but continued with heavy recklessness, 'The trouble with you is that your heart rules your head. It's a good fault sometimes but at others it robs the Public Prosecutor of a job. In this case, for instance, you've done it to such effect that you won't even look in the obvious place. I know you're touchy on the subject, that's why I didn't broach it before. But there comes a time—' he paused, appalled at his own temerity, but doggedly determined to go on. 'I've taken the trouble to have a house in Chelsea watched. On the two nights when the Shadow has done his job, a certain gentleman living in the said house has been out late. Very late. Late enough to have done the job. Mannering *is* the Shadow. When are you going to wake up to it, Bill?'

CHAPTER TWO

TOBY PLENDER

Mr. Tobias Plender, Q.C., had a large practice, a good reputation, a beautiful wife and plenty of money. Yet there were times when the look in his grey eyes was sombre. On the afternoon of the first day of March it was excessively so. He was sitting in his club, for he had lingered over lunch and there was nothing of pressing urgency in his chambers. The room, large, high and furnished in heavy reds and browns, overlooked the Mall.

Plender leaned back, his eyes hooded, his long, pale hands resting lightly on the arms of this chair. In front of him was a small table, and on it several evening papers, and the headlines about the Shadow's latest burglary were visible in all of them.

A solitary waiter, watching lynx-eyed for the crook of a finger which might summon him to the first club member who wanted tea, was startled when Plender, without warning or apparent premeditation, jumped to his feet and strode towards the door.

'Good-day, sir. Lovely day.'

'Foul,' said Plender, and moved on. He was tall, large-boned to the point of ungainliness, yet there was a curious ease about his movements. He went no further than the telephone booths, where he dialled a Chelsea number. Almost immediately a woman's voice answered him.

'This is Lorna Mannering.'

'And this is Toby Plender.'

'Toby! We haven't heard from you for ages.'

'I work,' said Plender. 'I can't afford to have the wife of a millionaire art dealer painting my portrait. I can't afford—'

Lorna was laughing.

'You're wrong again,' she said. 'I regret, no millionaire; no art dealer.'

'John is near enough to both,' said Toby. His voice low-pitched, held a touch of that magic with which he swayed the mind of jurors. 'How are you, my dear?'

'Fine.'

'Where's John?'

'At the shop, as far as I know.'

'That may not be far enough to keep him there until I arrive. Some myrmidon, bowing obsequiously will very much regret that he has just been called away, on pressing business. I know. I employ a few myrmidons out of the same box myself.'

'He'll be there,' said Lorna confidently. 'Toby, try and fix an evening together. All four, I mean, not just you and John. I'd love that.'

'I will not be painted,' stated Toby, with theatrical vehemence. 'All love, my dear.'

He rang off and stepped out of the telephone booth.

He frowned. Frowning, he was an impressive looking man. He nodded curtly to the porter at the great doors, and walked towards his car. He drove the massive black monster slowly towards the thicker traffic and, once there, beat two sets of traffic lights. It took him little more than ten minutes to reach New Bond Street. He parked it in a space vacated at the moment of his arrival, accepting his luck with the unconsciousness of a successful man.

His face was still grooved in seriousness as he walked towards a narrow street nearby, known as Hart Row. In Hart Row there were a few exclusive shops, which served the influential and the rich. In only one of these shops was a poor man genuinely welcome, but even there, he could not have found anything within his pocket's reach. This shop was the smallest of the few, narrow and single-fronted, with dark, oiled woodwork, and in gilt Old English lettering on the fascia board, the single word, *Quinns*.

In the window a Genoese silver table, breath-taking in its beauty, stood against a background of dark blue velvet. It was just possible to see beyond, into the long narrow shop. As Plender touched the handle, the door opened and a tall, silvery-haired man with the face of an archangel, bowed from the waist.

'Good afternoon, sir.'

'Good afternoon,' said Plender, his frown deepening, 'You're new, aren't you?'

'I have served Mr. Mannering for two years, sir.'

'Then either you've been out when I've called or I haven't called,' said Plender. 'It can't be two years! Plender—Mr. Toby Plender. Mr. Mannering will see me.'

'If you will please wait for *one* moment, sir.'

Alone, Plender had time to glance at a few of the pieces near at hand, caskets and cabinets, miniatures, vases—all precious and valuable things—before the man he had come to see appeared from the dim recess of the shop with outflung hands.

'Well, well!' Mannering said. 'I thought the next time I'd see you, you'd be leading the prosecution against me.'

'There's time,' said Plender. 'Well, John?'

'Brimming over.'

'Switzerland to blame?'

'I haven't set foot in Switzerland for three years,' Mannering said, and took the other by the arm and led him towards the rear of the shop. 'Don't disturb us, Sylvester,' he said to the white-haired man, who bowed his practised bow, and was at hand to close the door of a small office.

A small desk, its beauty hidden because of the narrowness of the space round it, was pushed close against the far wall. Behind it was a swivel armchair, of severe office mode, and two others, rather more comfortable. Filing cabinets, shelves crammed with large books and the shining knob of a combination safe, made up the furniture.

Plender rubbed the bridge of his nose, a gesture with which judges, jurors and jail-inmates all over England were familiar. His gaze raked the office, and came to rest finally on Mannering.

'Remarkable,' he said.

'What is?'

'The similarity. You only have to change the furniture, and you'd have a prison cell.'

'Homely,' Mannering said. 'Sit down.

Tea?'

'Thanks, later.' Plender accepted a cigarette. His eyes were still sombre, although his lips smiled. 'You really look younger,' he announced. 'It must be the Devil in you, he can invert the usual processes if he's so minded, so I'm told.'

'I wouldn't know,' said Mannering.

'Wouldn't you?' Plender leaned back in his chair and rubbed his nose again. Mannering's smile remained, but the glow of welcome had faded from his eyes. They appraised each other, two men who had once been close friends and who had drifted, more by accident and Plender's calling, than by design. They were about the same age, Plender at forty-one, a little older.

'You're wrong,' Mannering announced, at last.

'I doubt it. About what?'

'Whatever dark reasoning brought you here.'

Plender said abruptly: 'John, why do you do it? All this, I mean, and I don't mean the office.' He raised his eyebrows. 'The shop—daily grind—servitude, Regency period manners, a place steeped in the past and meant to be nostalgic. Why?'

'Modern business methods applied to my

job.'

'Lost all your money?'

'I am still what is referred to in certain government circles as a bloated capitalist.'

'So you don't need to run a shop?'

'For money, no. You wouldn't understand doing a thing for the love of it, would you?'

Plender chuckled.

'Your trick. You don't love being a counter-jumper, surely?'

'But Sylvester adores it. How can I disappoint him? Besides, I like the things I buy and sell. Not worrying whether I make a profit or not helps me to enjoy it. However, the profit is there.'

'Hum,' said Plender.

Mannering said: 'Toby, I told you how wrong you were—and you still are. Listen carefully.' He paused, and when the pause was almost unendurable, went on: 'I never did it, Guv'nor, so help me, I never did it. It's them perlice. Always arter me, they are, won't let a man earn a n'onest living.'

His voice changed, took on a nasal whine, and appeared to come from the side of his mouth; his lips hardly moved. He hunched his shoulders and put his head on one side, and somehow the gay and handsome man was no longer there, instead a scared yet malignant individual looked at Plender out of narrowed eyes.

He stopped; and became himself again.

Plender said; 'Exhibitionism. John, listen to me, we were once close friends. The reason we haven't seen much of each other is not that I know you were the Baron. Personally, I liked the bloke—as the Baron, I mean. But I prefer the legend to the fact. He died—remember?'

Mannering murmured: 'And you don't like his shadow.'

Plender stubbed out his cigarette. There was neither sound nor movement.

'I do not like his shadow,' he agreed at last.

'Why should you? He robbed you.' Mannering smiled without gaiety. He hesitated, and then said deliberately: 'That is one thing which makes me want to take a poke at you, Toby. Then we could make up and be friends. I was the Baron and you know it. The Baron did not rob his friends. If you want convincing proof that the Shadow is a shadow and not substance, that's it.'

Plender relaxed.

'No apology,' he said. 'I'd just moved. No one was to know that I lived in that house, or that my wife would lose her diamonds. You're not your own shadow?'

'I am not.'

'Not exactly my mistake,' said Plender. 'I feared rather than believed it. Ever thought of trying to catch this Shadow, John?'

Mannering eyed him levelly for some seconds, then smiled faintly, lifted the telephone and said: 'We'll have tea now, Sylvester,' and replaced the receiver with great deliberation; and all the time he watched Plender, who didn't shift his gaze. The receiver went ting. Mannering withdrew his hand, and drummed the fingers gently on the desk.

'Did Bristow send you?' he asked.

CHAPTER THREE

MANNERING INQUIRES

Plender laughed without answering, Mannering's smile broadened as he opened a drawer in the desk and took out a manilla folder. It was very like the one which had been on Anderson-Kerr's desk, but not so well-filled. He opened it and turned over the papers inside. Plender watched Mannering, not the papers.

'So Bristow did ask you to look in,' said Mannering.

'If he did, it was forgiving of him.'

'Sure?' Mannering took out several sheets of paper covered with type-written notes, and slipped it across the desk. 'There's hardly a job in which the Yard doesn't need an expert of one kind or another. Bill's up against the old brick wall. I can go to places where he can't, and a buyer of jewels will be trusted where a Yard man is always shown the door. In your hand, you hold a note of every job that the Shadow's done.'

Plender glanced down at it.

'So you're already working against him.'

'Oh, no,' said Mannering firmly. 'I've simply made lists of the stolen stuff, to make sure that I don't buy any, knowingly. It would never do if the Yard thought I was a fence, would it? With one possible exception, this is not a job that makes me want to go after the Shadow.'

'What's the exception?'

'The theft from Tobias Plender, Q.C. Not that I think he suffered so much, and he's doubtless done well out of insurance. The Shadow so far has been a polite and gentlemanly thief, catching him is a police job.'

'I thought you were poacher turned gamekeeper.'

'At times,' agreed Mannering. 'But I like to think it's worthwhile. Within these four walls, why should I go after a man for doing almost exactly what I once did myself? It would make me a renegade!' His eyes were gleaming, and Plender looked rueful. 'Now if the Shadow suddenly takes to violence, or steps outside his present limits, that would be a different kettle of fish. I—come in, Sylvester.'

There had been the lightest of taps at the door.

Sylvester brought in a tea tray, with the dignity and aplomb of the traditional butler, bowed, and went out.

'So I can take it you won't do anything about these jobs?' said Plender.

'Tell Bill I'm keeping a cousinly eye open,' said Mannering cheerfully. 'Also tell him there isn't any reason, so far, to think I can do much better than he has. The Shadow is good.'

'I suppose you're full of admiration for him,' said Plender dryly.

'He does a highly efficient job. Milk and sugar, isn't it? How's Mary. And the boys?'

Plender had three sons. . . .

Half an hour later, when he rose to go, Mannering put the file back into the drawer, and stood up.

'Just a minute, Toby.' They eyed each other, Plender expectantly. 'Any particular reason why you want to recover any of the jewels you lost?'

'There was a ruby pendant,' Plender said. 'It's been in the family for several generations, we were both attached to it. The insurance paid for it, but—'

'You might try one other thing,' suggested Mannering. 'Advertise in all the newspapers. Appeal to the Shadow's better nature. This pendant was of great sentimental value, your wife is pining for it, you know the kind of thing.'

'He'd never rise to that hoary bait.'

'He might,' said Mannering. 'It would give us a new slant on him, anyhow. Remember that behind everything else, he's building up a reputation. The public is getting almost fond of him. There's the vague personality emerging of a gentleman cracksman. It's probably spurious, and this might help to settle it one way or the other.'

'Could do,' said Plender dubiously. 'I'll think about it. John—'

'Yes?'

'Solemn word and all that kind of thing, you're not the Shadow?'

'My solemn word on it,' said Mannering.

'Subject dropped. Oh, Lorna said something about fixing a foursome. Will you both come and have dinner—one day next week?' Plender flipped over the pages of his diary. 'Wednesday would suit me, I think it's all right at home. Yes?'

'You might have the pendant back by then,' said Mannering. 'Yes—thanks, Toby.'

Mannering saw him to the door, and returned, pensively, to the office. Sylvester was talking earnestly to a prospective buyer who appeared to be interested in an Elizabethan casket, beautifully jewelled. Mannering sat back and closed his eyes, and was in that pose for nearly twenty minutes.

Presently he made his way to the four-hundred-year-old oak staircase, which he soberly mounted. On the next floor, narrow passages led to three store-rooms and a small room where one of the staff slept. On the floor above were more store-rooms, and a workshop in which an elderly, gentle-faced man was cleaning an old canvas. At sight of Mannering he put down the wad of cotton wool with which he was rubbing the picture, and smiled a welcome.

'How's it shaping up, Josh?'

'I'm not sure yet, Mr. Mannering. Mind you, it's old, very old. The varnish was nearly all worn off, and the paint itself in badly cracked and dirty condition. I don't want to do any damage—you might find it wise to send it to a restorer, Mr. Mannering—I'm only an amateur, you know.'

'You'd get a job with any restorer as an expert.' Mannering took the picture off the bench, and carried it to the window. In the patches which Josh Larraby had cleaned was something of the richness which one associated with the Dutch and Flemish masters. 'I think it's going to be good. Tired of working indoors, Josh?'

'I'm quite content,' said Larraby.

Mannering put the picture down carefully.

'I really believe you are! Know anything about the depredations of the Shadow?'

'Only what I hear in the street and read in the newspapers.'

'Try to pick up odds and ends of information about him, will you?' asked Mannering, his voice even, and without expression, 'One of his victims was an old friend of mine.'

'I'm sorry to hear that. I'll inquire, Mr. Mannering, but I don't really think I shall get any information of importance. Shall I leave everything else, and just get on to this?'

'No—fit it in, as you go along. Take what time you want for it.'

'Very good,' said Larraby. 'Are you thinking of investigating yourself?'

'Not yet.'

'It doesn't seem to me one of the inquiries which would greatly interest you,' said Larraby. There was an old-worldy air about the man, and his gentle voice and precise way of speaking added to it. 'I don't think the Shadow has a criminal background, he isn't one of the profession, so to speak. Or rather, I shall be surprised if it ever proves that he is.'

Mannering shrugged.

Just after six o'clock that evening, he drove

his Sunbeam Talbot to his lock-up garage in Chelsea and walked from there to his flat, in River Walk. The flat was on the top floor of a large house in a terrace. From the outside, it was ugly, inside there was little to recommend the main hall or the heavy staircase, but his own flat had an air which seemed to belong to a different world. He closed the front door and walked across to the living-room; it was empty. It had the charm which came from carefully selected pieces of furniture, none of them modern, except a radio-gram. One great window overlooked the river, and the lights of the Embankment and two bridges were reflected on the rippling surface; he didn't draw the curtains, but stood looking out. As he stood there, the door opened wider. Lorna Mannering came in.

She walked across the room without a word, and stood by his side. His arm went round her waist. They watched the distant river, the headlights glowing along the Embankment, the sharply contrasting outlines shown up in them. After a while, Lorna moved away and began to pull the curtains.

'Hetty never remembers,' she said. 'If she weren't a good cook, she'd be hopeless.'

'She's like you,' Mannering said. 'One in a million.'

'I thought you liked sentiment. Been busy?'

'Fairly. The light was just right, and I worked longer than I usually do.'

Mannering stood and looked at her. The subdued glow threw her features into soft relief. She was tall, her dark hair thick and wavy. There were those who said that, in repose, she looked grave; almost sullen, but none who argued that she wasn't beautiful.

Mannering switched on more lights. 'Don't overdo it. I happen to love you, in case you haven't noticed. Sherry?' He busied himself with bottles and glasses. 'Did Toby call up, this afternoon?'

'As a matter of fact, he did.'

'Dinner with him next Wednesday be all right?'

'Quite. Sherry, I think.' Lorna sat on the arm of a chair and he brought the drinks across. 'What did he want?'

'Am I the Shadow? And if I'm not the Shadow, will I help to catch the man who is? Bill Bristow is perplexed, and must be almost desperate, or he wouldn't have sent an unofficial envoy. To the grey of your eyes, my sweet!' He drank.

'And what are you going to do?' demanded Lorna.

'Nothing, yet. Well, nothing much. I've

asked Josh to keep his eyes and ears open. Having a man who knows his underworld is an advantage. Josh thinks the Shadow comes from high society. Toby isn't exactly sore about his own loss, but there's a pendant he'd rather like back. I advised him to advertise, asking the Shadow to oblige him!'

Lorna's repose went, her beauty became vivid.

'Seriously?'

'Seriously! I think he will, too. I was firm, my dear. Emphatic. The Shadow is a police job, there's no reason why dog should eat dog. Pity, though. If he'd knock someone over the head, I'd like to have a shot at him. I haven't played at being detective for a long time. Where shall we go for dinner tonight?'

'We're staying in,' said Lorna. 'Don't go after the Shadow, unless you really have to. He's too much like the past.' She forced a laugh. 'Darling, what does get into us? The minute I heard your key in the door, I knew there was something different. Perhaps it was because Toby telephoned, and he started me thinking about the Baron days. I had the ghastly feeling that time had gone back ten years, and Bristow was at your heels with a search warrant and a pair of handcuffs. They were bad days.'

'A mere point of view. There were others. Mine was one.'

Lorna said: 'Don't fool yourself. Not that we have to go back ten years to feel that Bristow's on the doorstep. He seems to pop up every few months. I wonder what would have happened if you two hadn't taken to each other?'

'He would have made life a little more difficult, and I wouldn't have been able to play the great detective so easily. Bill's all right, but as worried as hell over the Shadow. He must be feeling now pretty much the same as he felt during the Baron's heyday. Darling, we're glooming! We needn't. After dinner, we shall dance, and after we've gone to the Plenders, we'll have a few days in Paris. I ought to go over to the Rougement sale, anyhow, and you might be able to buy a new dress. Another drink?'

Lorna said: 'No. John, you're dying to go after the Shadow, aren't you?'

'The answer, for personal satisfaction only, and not in the capacity of a police stooge,' said Mannering, 'is yes.'

'I suppose you won't be satisfied until you know who he is,' said Lorna. 'And it's no use begging you not to. Be careful, my darling.'

CHAPTER FOUR

NEWS OF THE SHADOW

The door of the flat at Albemarle Mansions opened, soft wall lighting along the wide passage showed Mary Plender hurrying towards them in a silvery evening gown, and the maid standing on one side.

'Lorna, it's so good to see you. John, I thought you'd forgotten us.' The women touched cheeks, then Mary gripped Mannering's hand. 'You're more hopelessly handsome than ever.'

'No competition,' said Plender, coming from a room on the right. 'It's heartbreaking.' He took Lorna's hands and kissed her. The women, lingering over wraps, he led Mannering into a large, comfortable-looking room, pleasantly furnished with books, a Persian cat, and armchairs drawn up near the fire.

'Whisky?'

'Thanks. I'm still out of jail, you see,' Mannering said.

'Keep out. They're overcrowded. How is business?'

'Flourishing. I needn't ask you about

yours, I can read it all in the newspapers,' said Mannering. 'I suppose you know that you've talked at least two innocent men into jail in the past six months.'

'Don't you believe it. If they weren't guilty on that score, they were on some other count. The wheels of justice do their job.' Plender sipped. 'Any news of the Shadow?'

'He remains unknown, even in the lowest circles.'

'Meaning?'

'I have my spies. He's not pally with the professional burglar. Some of them are beginning to resent his existence, and the speeding up of police attention. If the Shadow's not careful, he'll have a civil war on his hands.'

Plender chuckled.

'He'll be careful. I've heard from him.'

Mannering put his glass down, but didn't speak. Plender went across to a book case and took out a folded copy of *The Times*. Marked round in pencil was an advertisement.

'I saw it,' said Mannering. 'The *Echo* and the *Record* took it up, and gave you quite a splash—didn't you see? Appeal to the Shadow, lashes of sentiment. What does Bristow say?'

'Nothing, yet.'

'Meaning, he probably disapproves,' said

Mannering. 'If the Shadow really wants to become popular, all he has to do now is to return that pendant. He'll probably demand that you send a statement to the Press about it, and—'

'Intuition, or a case of indentical minds,' said Plender lightly, 'for the Shadow has indeed promised to return the pendant, on one condition; that I inform the Press when I get it.'

'Well, well,' said Mannering, and laughed. He finished his whisky. 'I wouldn't mind another, Toby! So he's playing to the gallery. I had a feeling that he was doing that deliberately, from the beginning. In the popular phrase, you have to admire him, don't you? Details?'

'He has a nerve, certainly.'

'We knew that. Why, in particular?'

'He asked for a detailed note of my movements for the next three days, and told me that he'd see that the pendant was returned to me during that time. This,' added Plender, his hand quite steady with the whisky, 'is the third day. He knows that we'll be here until about ten o'clock, and that we're going on to the *Lulu* afterwards. Nice timing, for you, wasn't it?'

'How did he send the message?'

'Telephone, from a call-box.'

'Did he suggest that it might be a police trap?'

Plender chuckled. 'He said that if it turned out to be one, Mary wouldn't have a jewel to call her own, and probably no fur coat, either.'

'Did he ring up himself?'

'I fancy so.'

'Voice?'

'It would pass anywhere.'

'I'm beginning to get fond of the Shadow,' said Mannering. 'Does Mary know about it?'

'Yes.'

'Subject for dinner table talk,' said Mannering. 'Is there a back way into the flats, Toby?'

'The usual tradesman's entrance. Why?'

'I was thinking,' said Mannering dreamily, 'that would be the natural time to choose, while you and Mary were away dancing here tonight. Now if we all went out by the front door, and I slipped back through the tradesman's entrance, we might get a nice surprise.'

'You don't improve,' said Plender.

The women came in. Mary Plender was nearly as tall as her husband, deep-breasted, serene looking but by no means a beautiful woman. There was merriment in her eyes, reflecting real pleasure at this reunion.

'What have you two been conspiring about?' asked Lorna.

'You'd be surprised,' said Plender darkly.

They left Albemarle Mansions in Plender's car. The entrance to the big block of flats was brightly lit, the light spreading to the parked cars in the driveway and on to the tall, narrow houses on the opposite side of the street. Two or three people walked along and two cars passed, but there was no indication that anyone was watching. Plender drove to Piccadilly, and then took a narrow turning which led, eventually, to the *Lulu*, a Soho club basking in the approval of the police and Mayfair society.

'Where are you going to get out?' Plender asked.

'On second thoughts, I'll come to the club,' said Mannering. 'The Shadow might be ultra careful, and not only make sure that we leave the flat but also that we're having a wonderful time. I'll disappear fairly early.'

'You could forget all about it,' suggested Lorna.

'Some other night,' said Mannering.

Dancing was in full swing. Unlike most night club's the *Lulu* had a comfortable floor space, and there was ample room to move about. The proprietress came hurrying towards them, as they entered.

'Mr. Plender, how lovely! And you didn't tell me that you'd be bringing Mr. and Mrs. Mannering, that makes it even more wonderful!' Her smile, though professional, was warm and pleasing. She touched Mannering's arm with a beringed hand. 'You ought to come and see us more often.'

'That's what my wife says, Lulu.'

'Well, now you're here, I've a *delightful* table for you. I don't think we're going to be *too* crowded tonight.'

Mannering said in a low voice: 'Just one small thing, Lulu—I want a telephone message, in about twenty minutes time, and I want you to say, quite loudly, that it's from Quinns, and there's been some trouble there. I'll have to go, but I'll be back before the night's out. Will you fix it?'

Without asking for the message to be repeated, Lulu nodded. She allowed time for one waltz, and then delivered it, making sure that the people at nearby tables heard that there was 'trouble' at Quinns. Most of the people there had already identified Mannering, many knew Quinns, none was surprised to see him hurry out.

He took a taxi to Berkeley Square, and then walked briskly towards Albermarle Mansions. As he walked, he felt the heady rise of excitement. He knew that the result of the ruse might be disappointing, but there was stimulation in the thought that this was the beginning of a hunt. It brought nostalgia, for the days of the Baron, when he would have slipped away from the *Lulu Club* on a more daring mission that this—a job such as the Shadow might do.

He reached the end of Bray Street. He saw no one. He had to walk a further few yards before turning off, towards the back entrance. He reached it, and surprised an elderly man, who was sitting reading a newspaper by the side of a big central heating boiler.

'Evening, sir.' The man put the newspaper down. 'Anything I can do for you?'

'I want to go in the back way,' said Mannering, and a ten shilling note appeared in his hand, as if by magic. 'A trick on Mr. Plender.' He beamed.

'Well, sir—'

'He'll be happy,' said Mannering.

There had been a time when it would have been vital to get past the night watchman without being seen; bribing his way took the edge off his enjoyment. He smiled to himself as he walked up the narrow, cemented stairs which led to the second floor and the main staircase. No one was about, and the lift was silent. He reached the Plender's flat—Number 14—and let himself in with Toby Plender's key.

A light glowed along the first passage; the maid was in, and knew he would be back. Plender had vouched for her loyalty.

Mannering went along to the door, and tapped before opening it. The maid, sitting in front of an electric fire, was knitting; and the Persian cat was sitting on her lap.

'Don't disturb him,' said Mannering. 'You know exactly what to do, don't you?'

'Oh, yes, sir. If anyone comes, I'm to let them come in, if they want to, and show them into the drawing-room. They're not to know that anyone else is at home. I'm to shut the door, if they *do* come in, and then come back here.'

'And if they stay outside?'

'I'm to detain them for a few minutes if I can.'

'That's fine,' said Mannering.

He went back to the drawing-room. There was a door leading to the small dining-room, which stood ajar. He went across and opened it two or three times; there was no squeak. He went into the dining-room and found that he could see into the room through the crack between the door itself and the frame. Next he went into the hall. There was a tall wardrobe, standing near the front door and there was room for a man to hide behind it. He stepped inside, his hair ruffled by coats, and closed it on himself. He couldn't see through the keyhole. He opened the door a shade; he could see the front hall, but anyone standing in the doorway could see him. He decided to stay in the dining-room all the time.

It was a little after eleven o'clock.

He selected *Paradise Lost* in a tooled leather binding, went into the dining-room and switched on a standard lamp, and began to read; the beauty of the words, was like the company of an old friend.

His blood pounded with an upsurge of exhilaration.

A clock struck the half hour. If the Shadow was a man of his word, he or a messenger would be here within thirty minutes unless he decided to be spectacular and return the pendant at the *Lulu*. If that happened Mannering wouldn't live this down for a long time.

Another ten minutes passed—and then he heard the front door bell ring.

He put the book down and switched off the light. He heard voices, but at first couldn't be sure whether the caller was man or woman. Then he heard the maid say 'Mr. Plender's out, I'm afraid, but if you would like to leave a message. . . .'

A girl said: 'Oh, no, I won't trouble. But—do you know where I might find Mr. Plender?'

'He's out dancing, *some*where.'

'Oh,' said the girl, who had a pleasant voice. 'I'm sorry I've missed him, but will you please give him this?'

CHAPTER FIVE

MAN OF HIS WORD

Mannering slid into the hall as the front door closed. The maid had a small package in her hand.

'She wouldn't come in, sir.'

'That's all right.' Mannering took the packet and slipped it into his pocket. 'Switch the light off until I've gone, will you?' As the light went out, he opened the door and stepped into the wider passage beyond. He could hear no sound of footsteps. The Shadow's messenger wasn't in sight. He hurried to the landing, and pressed the lift button. The lift arrived almost at once, and he reached the ground floor as a girl walked across the big, carpeted hall. A porter, in uniform, said:

'Good night.'

'Good night, thank you.'

The girl sounded young and timid. Mannering stepped unnoticed out of the lift, He saw her clearly against the brighter light. She was well-dressed, and walked easily. He reached the door as she stepped into a waiting taxi.

'The Grand Palace Hotel,' she said to the driver.

'Okay, Miss.'

Mannering was already at the Sunbeam Talbot. The engine started at a touch, and before the taxi was out of Bray Street, he was on the move. The taxi turned right, towards Piccadilly; it would go on to the Circus, to reach the Grand Palace Hotel, which was almost within walking distance. Without hurrying, Mannering kept the cab in sight. It reached Piccadilly Circus, but instead of turning left to the hotel turned into Haymarket.

'They're careful,' Mannering murmured; and laughed to himself. He followed to Trafalgar Square, then across the Strand to the Adelphi. The taxi took several turnings in that quiet backwater off the main thoroughfare, and pulled up halfway along a narrow street of residential houses. Mannering drove to the end, returning on foot. The girl was standing by the side of the taxi, in the shadow.

He heard the taxi driver laugh.

The girl turned into a house; the seventh on the right-hand side of the street. The cab turned. Mannering hurried back to his car, and was facing the same direction as the taxi when it appeared again. Its hire sign was down, but Mannering saw no passenger. It turned towards the Embankment and stopped at the first set of traffic lights. Several cars and taxis were between it and Mannering when they started off again. At Blackfriars Bridge, the taxi turned right, and then rattled over the bridge towards Southwark. It was stopped again at traffic lights and a few hundreds yards along, turned off the main road. Mannering didn't follow, but stopped the car. A constable came along towards him.

Mannering called: 'Can I park here, constable?'

'How long for, sir?'

'Oh, half an hour or so.'

'That's all right, sir, at this time of night.'

He went off with the Juggernaut tread of the traditional policeman, and Mannering turned in to one of the lighted doorways. He didn't stay, but walked to the road which the taxi had taken. He found himself in a rabbit warren of sparsely lighted narrow streets, between tall warehouses. Walking on, he came presently to an all-night cafe. The eyes of four solitary customers turned to him with veiled suspicion as he went in. The proprietor, a meek-looking man with a walrus moustache, came bustling towards him on the other side of the counter.

'Any cigarettes?' asked Mannering. 'They told me I might be lucky, here.'

'Got a few *Players*, if they'll do, sir.'

'Thanks. And a cup of tea.'

Mannering, waiting for the tea and cigarettes, looked casually round the almost empty cafe. 'Hardly worth your while opening all night, is it?' he asked with the air of a man pleasantly and unimportantly filling a pause.

'You'd be surprised. There's a lot of work at the warehouses by night. There're a couple of all-night garages, too. Our job's to serve the public, that's my motto.'

'It couldn't be better. Anywhere I can get a taxi?'

'Several places,' the man said promptly. 'Nearest is straight on, first right, then it's at the next corner. Only a little place, but there's always someone on duty at night. Anything else I can do for you, sir?'

'No, thanks, that was good.' Mannering went out, nodding to the suspicious quartette, and sauntered to the end of the road. None of the men came out to watch him. He walked briskly to the corner. The main entrance to the taxi-garage was in a side street. Two men were talking in a dim light, one of them in shirt sleeves, the other in muffler and coat. Mannering saw both men vividly; the first plump, the other with a face which was hatchet thin. He thought it was the driver of the girl's taxi. He walked past, glancing inside and saw the taxi. He recognised both the shape and the registration number.

The two men watched him without expression.

He walked on to the main road and back to his own car. No one approached, and no one had followed. Was he taking a lot of precautions for nothing? It could be, but it wasn't until he was on the other side of Blackfriars Bridge that he felt quite free from the risk of surveillance.

He was at *Lulu's* before one o'clock.

*   *   *

'John,' said Lorna, from her bed.

'Not asleep?' It was four o'clock, and they had been home for over an hour.

'What happened tonight?'

'I followed a girl to an address in Buckley Street and a taxi to Southwark. I fancy both know something about the Shadow.'

'Why did you tell Toby that you didn't

have any luck?'

'Because if I had, he'd probably tell Bristow. No reason why he shouldn't, no reason why I should ask him to keep it to himself, after all. Mary has her pendant back, so Toby should be happy. Or Mary should.'

'What are you going to do next?'

'Come and help you go to sleep,' said Mannering, and pushed back the bedclothes.

* * *

Two days later, towards evening, Larraby arrived at Quinns and paused in the open doorway of the office, to say that he thought he had some information that would be of interest. Mannering gave him five minutes, and then followed him. Larraby was standing in front of the little picture, which was now clean except in one corner.

'I feel sure it *is* a Rubens, sir.'

'Probably. What do you know, Josh?'

'Well,' said Larraby, with indirectly expressed triumph, 'I discovered that the garage behind the Southwark Road changed hands recently. It was up for sale six or seven months ago, and was bought by a man new to the London taxi business. He said he'd had a lot of experience in the Midlands, and brought his own staff with him—two mechanics and a clerk. He employs London drivers, of course, but there's one *very* interesting thing, sir.'

'What?'

'He's taken out a licence himself, and started to drive. He was out in the cab you saw, on Wednesday night. I got all of this in a roundabout way from one of the drivers he employs. He—that is, the proprietor—is a tall, thin man. He isn't popular, although he pays well. Too big for his boots. He doesn't go there regularly, though, leaves the management to one of the men he brought with him.'

'What's his name?'

'Caton—CATON. The other information makes it particularly interesting,' said Larraby, warming to his story. 'At Number 13, Buckley Street, the three separate flats have all been rented by the same man. He lives on the top floor, has an office on the bottom floor, and a kind of warehouse on the middle floor. He's a single man, but has two people sharing the flat with him—the girl, who seems to run the place, and an older woman. The girl's name is Caton, but the man's name is Smith.'

'Ah,' said Mannering, absently. 'And Smith is tall and thin, with a sardonic manner.'

'That is so,' said Larraby. 'I don't think there is much doubt that Smith and Caton are the same. The business is general mail order, they deal in small electrical appliances. It can't be a very big business, as he only employs five on the staff, in addition to the two women. I haven't been able to find out anything more, except that he appears to live in considerable style. Do you think these people are associated with the Shadow?'

'Yes, Josh. The mail order angle is interesting, too. Tired of the jobs?'

'Not if you think it's significant enough to follow up.'

'Sooner or later there will be fun with the Shadow,' said Mannering. 'Keep an eye on the Buckley Street house for a few nights, and telephone me if they all go out. It might be worth looking round.'

'And could be a little risky, sir.'

Mannering laughed.

'I know you don't regard risks as important, but is the Shadow worth it?' asked Larraby. 'It isn't your usual practice to—'

'Josh,' said Mannering, 'the Shadow is a jewel thief and a good one. He's been going the pace, but only on small stuff. He's been building up to something bigger, and we'll probably be very glad to know all we can about him. Right?'

'As you say,' murmured Larraby. 'Is your projected Paris trip off, Mr. Mannering?'

'Sadly, yes. Mrs. Mannering's mother is ill, and I'm a grass widower from now on. In fact there could hardly be a better time for the Buckley Street household to go out for a night, could there?'

'I'll see what I can do, sir,' said Larraby, smiling.

At a quarter past eight on the following evening, Mannering sat drinking coffee and looking through a small selection of books on the paintings of Rubens. If he could see the print he wanted, he would know he'd made a find. He was lost in the search when the telephone bell rang.

Mannering stretched out for it, his attention sharply focused as he heard Larraby's voice.

'They're out, sir, left in a taxi, five minutes ago.'

'Wonderful, I'll be there as soon as I can. It'll be the better part of an hour. Don't expect to recognise me, and keep out of sight until I turn up. Will you be near that house that's just being demolished?'

'Just inside the front doorway,' promised

Larraby.

Mannering went into the bedroom, took out a make-up set and spread out everything he wanted to use, took off his suit and, with a towel round his shoulders, set to work. Nostalgia gripped him as he worked in the grease paint. He was back at the day when he had first learned the art of make-up. He worked slowly at first, then more swiftly. After twenty minutes he leaned forward in careful scrutiny.

The change was fantastic. He looked ten years older. No one who knew him would recognise him, even under the most critical examination; that was all he wanted, for tonight. To finish the change, he inserted rubber cheek pads and worked a thin rubber covering over his teeth, altering his whole expression. He put on an old suit, padded at the waist, to make him look fatter, packed tools in a belt that would roll up or go right round his waist, and put money and a torch into his pockets. That done, he slipped unobtrusively out of the flat, ambling towards King's Road, took a bus to Victoria, and from there went to a lock-up garage where, in the name of Brown, he kept a powerful Buick.

Not only did he look a different man; he felt one.

He drove swiftly towards the Strand, left the Buick a hundred yards from Buckley Street, and walked the rest of the distance.

Number 13 was in darkness, but there were lights at the windows of the houses on either side.

The only street lamp was at the far end of the short street. There, a short flight of steps led to the lower level of Villiers Street and the Embankment. Just past the steps was a house in process of being demolished. He reached the steps, and glanced towards the house but saw no one.

He went nearer the doorway.

'All right, Josh,' he called.

There was no answer. The only sound was the traffic in nearby streets and, further away, the rumble of a train over Charing Cross Bridge. It was gloomy here, and gloomier inside the doorway of the house. He frowned as he went towards it, and stopped just outside.

'You there, Josh?'

There was no answer.

He put one hand in his pocket, and his fingers closed about the handle of a cosh. He gripped it tightly as he went nearer the doorway. If Larraby was there, he was within earshot; there was no legitimate reason why he shouldn't answer.

Mannering reached the doorway, and whispered: 'Josh.'

Silence met him.

He heard footsteps, and slipped quickly to one side, outside the shell of the building, but invisible from the street. A man and a woman walked briskly towards the steps, the woman talking; they clattered downward, the sound fading until there was only the muttering of traffic in the background and, nearer at hand, the sudden burst of a car engine starting up.

Mannering took out a torch, very gently playing the hooded beam.

'Josh,' he called, but in this last cry, he expected no answer. The night was cold—he shivered involuntarily. The beam of the torch shone on the rubble of bricks and mortar, and on a wheel-barrow, tilted on its side. The far wall of the house was still standing, but the roof was open to the skies. He half expected to see Larraby on the ground; if Larraby hadn't been attacked, why wasn't he here, answering?'

He turned round, slowly, not seeing what he feared.

A man struck at him from the other side of the doorway. The first blow caught him on the side of the head, the second under the chin. He sprawled back, without a chance to defend himself, then fell heavily.

Nearby, a man laughed.

CHAPTER SIX

THE MAN WHO LAUGHED

The laughter had a sinister note; there was no humour in it. The sound pierced Mannering's hazy consciousness. He tried to sit up, but a hand pressed against his shoulder and he was thrust heavily back. In the beam of a torch, he saw a pair of dusty shoes, quite near him.

'Don't move,' a voice cautioned. 'Just have a little rest.'

The laugh came again; sardonic, unpleasant.

Before the stillness had settled down into an uneasy vacuum in which it was possible to believe that any evil thing might fall, the slow throb of a car was heard. Mannering saw one of the shoes move.

'Get up,' the voice said.

Mannering struggled to his feet, and as he did so, his right hand was grabbed and held behind him.

'Forward,' the man ordered.

Outside, a taxi stood waiting, and near it a shadowy figure lurked in the doorway. Someone spoke, but Mannering didn't catch the words. He was pushed roughly into the cab. A man climbed in after him, and the door slammed. Mannering, huddled in a corner, eased his arm gently. The cab moved off, and they passed beneath the light of the single street lamp. He didn't catch more than a glimpse of his captor, whose hat was pulled low over his forehead, and whose chin and mouth were covered with a scarf; but he saw enough to note that the man was thin and rakish looking.

Something pressed into his side.

'That's a gun,' the man said.

Mannering made no comment.

'At least you don't talk too much. Who's Josh?'

Mannering kept silent.

'But you've got to learn to talk enough,' the man said. He held his hand out. 'Cigarette?'

Mannering grunted: 'No.'

'Pity,' the man said. 'It's doped—not enough to kill but enough to send you to sleep. I'll have to fix you the hard way.' He laughed again—and next moment Mannering felt a sharp prick in his thigh. He felt the plunger forced home, and shivered. 'If you behave yourself, you'll live,' the man said. 'Now just shut your eyes—when you wake up, you'll get a nice surprise.'

* * *

Mannering saw the light, not bright, but enough to make him blink and to bring tears of pain to his eyes. He closed them quickly. Except for a slight pain in his right arm, he felt no ill-effects of the encounter. He could think clearly; he recalled exactly what had happened up to the time he had felt sleep creeping over him, in the taxi.

No one moved or spoke.

After a few minutes, he opened his eyes and kept them open. He was in a small bedroom. In one corner was an old-fashioned double bed, with round brass knobs at the posts. There was a wash-stand with a marble top, a chest of drawers and a curtained window, and two small chairs with wicker seats. He lay opposite the door, in a large armchair; at least it was comfortable. He was able to keep his eyes open without much strain, now, but apart from the poor furnishings, there was nothing to see.

Experimentally he got up, and was relieved to find that after a first rock or two he stood firm.

He moved to the door. Several feet away,

he could see the shoddily fitted lock. He slipped his hand into his pocket for his knife, and it came out empty. Everything had been taken away, tools, money, even his loose change. He glanced about the room, but there was nothing he could use as a pick-lock.

He went back to the chair, and sat down.

His watch was gone too. He was glad it was unidentifiable. He stretched out his legs, and wished that he had a cigarette. Listening intently he could hear no sound about the house.

He went across to the window, and pulled aside the curtain. There were wooden shutters, fastened by iron brackets to the wall; there was no way in which he could open them, without tools.

He closed his eyes again, and began to think back over what had happened. The obvious reconstruction was likely to be the right one. Larraby had been seen watching, had been shanghaied. If he had undergone the same treatment as Mannering, Larraby was all right; for the time being.

Mannering's mind worked restlessly. He could search the room, and perhaps find something with which to unpick the lock, but at this stage, he didn't want to do that. Unless Josh had given his true identity away, and that wasn't likely, there was no way in which these people could find out who he was.

It had happened at a good time, too. Lorna wouldn't be waiting anxiously at home.

He heard a faint sound; as of metal on metal. He looked at the door through his lashes. There had been no footsteps nothing to indicate that anyone was outside, but the sound was repeated. Then he saw the handle of the door turning. Immediately he lowered his eyelids. The door opened—and a man said in a quiet but normal voice:

'He's still out.'

'Just go and make sure,' said the voice of Mannering's captor. 'He may be foxing.'

'Not on your life.' The first man's voice had a Midland accent with an overtone of Cockney. Mannering kept his eyes closed and his breathing even. He heard the others approach, and steeled himself for whatever test they were going to apply. He felt something touch his leg; next moment there was a sharp prick, as of a pin. He couldn't stop himself from a slight reaction, but his face remained expressionless.

'Satisfied now?' asked the man with the Midland accent.

'You go downstairs,' the other said. 'I'll wait until he comes round.'

'Taking a chance, aren't you?'

'Not with this.' The speaker sat on the bed, judging from the noise of groaning springs. Then there was the scrape of a match and a moment later, the smell of tobacco smoke. Springs creaked again; the man was probably lying on the bed. With infinite caution Mannering lifted his lids an eighth of an inch. The man was lying flat on his back, looking at him.

Mannering opened his eyes wider. The other was smiling, and it was easy to understand why he wasn't liked. Even smiling, there was a mocking look about him. He had a long, thin face, and a well-defined chin, and could be a type, Mannering thought, that was attractive to women. Lying there, he looked very tall.

'These aren't doped,' he said.

'Thanks.' Mannering didn't get up.

The man took out a cardboard carton of cigarettes and tossed them across; they fell on to Mannering's lap. A box of matches followed.

'Thanks,' said Mannering again. He lit a cigarette and tossed both matches and packet back. His voice was hoarse, the word had been little more than a croak. He was silently rehearsing the way to talk in a low-pitched voice unlike his own. It was a long time since he had found a use for an assumed voice.

'Still not talkative, I see.'

'No.'

'You'll learn. Before you leave here, I'm going to find out who you are. And if necessary, I'll make your boy-friend wish he hadn't been foolish enough to work for you. Why were you watching me?'

Mannering said: 'I was—' and then broke off.

The other swung his legs off the bed and came across, put his hand beneath Mannering's chin, and forced his head up. From that angle, the lean face had an almost savage look; this man could be merciless.

His voice was gentle but there was menace in it.

'Listen, mister, I'm serious. I can wipe that grease-paint off and take a pretty picture of you, and that won't help you to keep yourself anonymous. Even if you're stubborn, it won't help. But I don't want to hurt you for the sake of it. What were you doing?'

Mannering licked his lips.

'I thought—'

'Go on, get it out.'

'I thought it would be an easy job.'

'What would?'

'Breaking in.'

'What did you want from my place?'

Mannering said: 'I had a van coming, we could have cleared you out. Always got a ready market for electrical stuff.' He licked his lips again. Pretending to be nervous helped him to put over the assumed voice; helped also to make the 'confession' sound convincing.

The man stood back, the sardonic twist of his lips more pronounced than ever.

'Why didn't you tell me the first time?'

'Pretty obvious, isn't it?'

'Did you think I'd turn you over to the police?'

'Aren't you—' Mannering leaned forward, and allowed a hopeful calculation to creep into his eyes. 'Aren't you going to? I won't try the job again, I'll keep away, you won't have to worry—'

'That's right,' the other said. 'You'll have to do the worrying. Tell me all about yourself, mister—what kind of job you do, how long you've been at it, how many friends are in your racket. Just a potted autobiography and be quick about it.'

He went back to the bed and sat down, waiting expectantly.

CHAPTER SEVEN

OFFER

The great danger would come from Larraby. If he were forced to talk, his story would be different from anything Mannering said. Larraby would talk only under great pressure, but though the man here had used the kid gloves so far, there was no guarantee he would continue to do so.

He sat there, leaning against the head of the bed, the smile curling his lips.

'Well?'

Mannering moistened his lips.

'I've been in the game for years. I haven't got a record, I've been to careful. Forced entry to empty places and lifted the stuff—small stuff, like you keep. It sells quick, no one knows whether it's hot. I've got my own trade channels.' There was another danger, that his natural speaking voice would break through the assumed tone; only a word or two, wrongly uttered, would be sufficient to make this man suspicious. Mannering's mouth was dry, and he paused frequently. That helped the story to sound realistic and gave him time to articulate carefully. 'I never use the same fence for long, it's too dangerous. I have the place watched before I do the job—'

'Who does the forcing?'

'I do.'

'Are you good?'

'They don't come any better,' said Mannering.

'What does your friend Josh do?'

'Keeps a look out. He's safe. He hasn't got much sense, but he's reliable.'

'How long have you been watching me?'

Mannering hesitated, and then said slowly: 'About two weeks, altogether. Didn't do it every night, at first. As soon as I decided to have a cut at your place, I put Josh on every night. He was to tell me when you was all out.'

'How did you get on to me?'

Mannering gave a little sniggering laugh, as if his confidence were returning.

'You wouldn't be the first mail order place I've done, not by a long way.'

'I hope you've been telling me the truth,' the man said. He stood up, slowly; the sinuous movement was like a thick snake, uncoiling; there was something in his expression that suggested he was going to strike, and there would be poison in his fangs. He came to Mannering and thrust his head up roughly. 'It had better be true.'

He swung round, and went out. The key grated in the lock.

Mannering sat where he was, dabbing at his forehead with a handkerchief. It hadn't been good, but this was the worst, for Larraby was almost certainly being questioned. He waited until his hands steadied, then crossed to the bed. The creaking sound suggested that there were broken springs. He lifted the mattress. In the corner he uncovered there were several broken pieces of wire, one nearly four inches long. He moved it to and fro until it snapped. He bent the head of the wire at right angles to the main piece. Then he crouched in front of the door, and began to insert it. The faint scratching sounded over-loud.

He could hear nothing else; no traffic; nothing to suggest this was near a busy road. He would have welcomed any noise then.

He could have had this lock forced in twenty seconds with a proper instrument. Now, minutes ticked by, until at last the wire held fast. Would it be strong enough to turn? He held the end with a handkerchief, and twisted gently, afraid that it would slip or break.

The lock rasped back.

His heart jumped as he waited, listening intently. There was still no sound, nothing to suggest that the noise had been heard. He turned off the electric light, easing the switch against a sudden click. Then he turned the handle and opened the door an inch.

A dim light showed a landing and the head of a flight of stairs. He opened the door wider. He could see no one, unless a man stood close to the well, no one was there. He was prepared for a sudden attack as he sidled out, but none came; and soon he could see the whole of the landing. He had been left unguarded.

He could hear a murmur of voices, now, and crept down the stairs, keeping close to the wall. Even with that precaution the treads creaked. He reached the next landing and saw a streak of light beneath a door, on his left. There was a lighted hall below, narrow and dingy looking. Against one wall was a hall stand, and in it, two umbrellas and a walking-stick. He went down the next flight still keeping close to the wall. He picked up the walking-stick, then opened the front door. He could smell petrol; this was a garage, and probably the garage near Southwark Street.

He hurried back upstairs. The murmuring of voices was still going on. As he reached the door, it stopped. He turned the handle, and pushed; the door wasn't locked.

The sardonic man said:

'You'll get hurt if you don't talk, Josh. Your Boss wouldn't like that, would he?'

There was no answer; trust Josh!

Mannering thrust the door open and stepped inside.

★ ★ ★

Larraby stood in a corner, with a man behind him, holding his right arm in a hammer lock. The sardonic man was in front of Josh. A cigarette drooped from the corner of his lips. For the first second, no one stirred.

The man behind Josh, too astonished to know what exactly was happening, released his hold.

'That's better,' Mannering said in the new harsh voice. 'Take it easy, all of you.' He strode to a table and leaned against it.

It was a deal table, laid for a meal at one end. On the other end were the things taken from Mannering's pockets. The tool waistbelt was unrolled, but intact. Mannering picked everything up, watched by the tall man. His face didn't fit into any category easily; the word that sprang to Mannering's mind was satanic.

This was a kitchen, with an old-fashioned dresser, several kitchen chairs, and a cooking stove.

'So you *are* good,' said the sardonic man.

'Sure, Smith, I'm good.' There was swagger in Mannering's manner, gloating in his voice. 'There isn't a lock that can keep me inside, if I want to get out. And *vice versa*. Have they hurt you, Josh'

Larraby said: 'No—no, Gov'nor.'

'Told them anything?'

'Not a word, Guv'nor, I swear—'

'It's okay, but you could have done, I told them all they need to know.' Mannering laughed. 'Not feeling so good now, Smith, are you?'

Smith shrugged. 'One move of the game is not the whole show.'

Mannering said: 'That's the point. I don't know what your game is, but I do know it's not mail order. Let's have the truth. Mail order's a cover—what's your line?'

'The same as yours,' said Smith laconically.

'So it's the same as mine.' Mannering laughed. 'Maybe we ought to get together.'

'That's what I was thinking,' said Smith. 'If you're as good at cracking a crib as you are at opening a door, we ought to be able to form a partnership.'

'We'll see,' said Mannering. 'Just get one thing into your thick head, Smith. I can bust any lock. They don't make them so hard that they can keep me out. Isn't that so, Josh?'

Larraby licked his lips.

'You're a wonder, Guv'nor, a perishing wonder.' His voice was pitched to a whining note, the calm dignity which as part of him at *Quinns* lost in a cringing obsequiousness.

'If you're so good as that, why waste time with my stuff?' Smith sneered. 'You're just a piker.'

'I play safe,' said Mannering.

'Maybe.' Smith's manner was exactly the same as it had been upstairs, the turn of the tables hadn't affected him outwardly. 'I could use a good screw.'

'*You* could use one, could you? I don't go into any job working for anyone else, *Mister* Smith, get that straight. Maybe I'd go fifty-fifty, but it's only maybe. If you want to talk business, make an appointment—with Mr. Brown, Post Office, Strand—the Trafalgar Square end. Josh, we're going to get out of here.'

Smith moved. 'Listen—'

'You heard,' Mannering said.

Josh slipped past the man. The other, more than a little out of his depth, had stayed where he was. He didn't move now. Mannering backed to the door. Smith made no further attempt to stop him. Mannering covered Josh as he slipped out. Quickly following, he turned the key in the lock.

'Wonderful!' breathed Josh.

'Not yet,' said Mannering. 'Stay outside until they get free. Try and get a close up of everyone who comes to the front door or to the garage. We're near Southwark Street. Don't let them catch you again, and keep away from Quinns until this is all over, they might find out where you work otherwise. All clear?'

'But—'

'Stay at a hotel near Quinns and let me know which it is,' said Mannering. 'I'll be seeing you.'

He ran down the stairs and out into the street. It was as he had thought, the same garage, and the man in the kitchen was the man he had seen standing there in his shirt sleeves. He hurried towards one of the larger garages, and five minutes after leaving the house, was in a taxi, humming towards Blackfriars Bridge. Little more than ten minutes later, he was standing by the side of his Buick, near Buckley Street. He paid off the driver, and waited until the cab had disappeared. Then he headed for Number 13, Buckley Street. He had a knife in his hand, one with some remarkable blades; with one, he opened the front door almost as quickly as if he had a key for the Yale lock.

There was no light on; and there had been none at the windows.

He found himself in a wide hall, with a passage running alongside a narrow staircase; there was a door at the end of the passage. It was unlocked, and he walked through an office. Another door led to a kitchen which had been turned into a stationery store room, although the gas stove was still in service, and there were cups and a teapot on the table. The back door was locked and bolted; he opened it, and left it latched, then returned quickly to the staircase. The only sound was that of his own movements. Although he was sure that the house was empty, he went up cautiously. Several rooms led off the first landing, all of them were store rooms filled with boxes. He went up to the next flight of stairs, groped for and found the light, and looked about him.

It was obviously the landing of two flats. But each, rather strangely, had the same number: 3. He turned to the nearer door, and took out the knife.

There was one disadvantage about forcing a Yale lock; once damaged, you couldn't close the door securely again. He closed it as best it would go, and then switched on a light.

He was in a small, comfortably furnished room. There were water colours on the walls, a standard lamp, books in corner fittings, several easy chairs and a thick carpet. Three rooms led from it. He explored each in turn. There was a book-lined study, a bedroom and a bathroom; and all obviously belonged to a man. In the study beneath a rack of pipes, golf clubs were reared up against a corner. It was a comfortable, pleasant room, but he was in no mood to be beguiled. He moved the several oil paintings, but failed to expose the expected wall safe. The only piece of furniture which might conceal what he was looking for was the desk. It was large, almost too large for the room. Behind it was a comfortable chair. He sat in the chair, and studied the drawers of the desk. Then he pulled them out, one after the other; each was the same length, about two feet; but the desk was nearly four feet across.

Walking round it, he studied the back. Tapping it sharply it gave off a keen, unwooden sound. He straightened up, smiling faintly.

The back of the desk was of metal almost certainly steel. The desk *was* the safe.

He examined the top surface more closely. It was made out of two pieces of wood, and the join was permanent. He examined the carving at the edges, pressing here and there, but discovered nothing. Then he found screws, at each corner, cunningly concealed by the carving itself. He used the screw-driver blade.

When the screws were out, the top of the desk could be moved. It wasn't so heavy as he had expected. Beneath it was a layer of oak, fitted with hinges at one side and a lock at the other. Picking that lock would take some time. He glanced at his watch. He had been here for over half an hour. It was nearly an hour since he had left the garage. There was no certainty that Smith or Caton would come straight here, but he might. Mannering left the desk as it was, and went across to the door, listening. He heard nothing, but a keen awareness of danger caused him to push the door open.

A girl stood in the middle of the hall, covering him with a gun.

CHAPTER EIGHT

THE GIRL

She was young and strikingly attractive.

She wore a dark dress, with lace at the neck and cuffs; absurd things to notice, but he noticed them. Her glossy dark hair dropped to her shoulders, curling inwards at the ends. The gun, a small automatic, was steady in her hand.

'Go to the corner by the lamp,' she said, 'and don't try to be clever.'

The voice was calm and untroubled, and he had heard it before; she was the girl who had taken the pendant to Plender's flat. He obeyed her, backing step by step.

The door behind her was ajar.

Near it, was a telephone. Keeping him covered, she lifted the receiver with her free hand. He heard the faint burring sound.

'Do you know of any good reason why I shouldn't send for the police?'

Mannering said: 'Yes, I do.'

'What is it?'

'There's more than a chance that it might seriously annoy Smith.'

She started, and her forefinger moved away from the dial. Mannering watched her eyes. She wasn't frightened, but suddenly she had become a little less certain of procedure.

'You don't know him.'

'Don't I?' asked Mannering. 'He knows me, anyway, and before I leave here, I'm going to know a lot more about him. Him and his—shadow.'

He dropped the word out, sharply. He expected her to show reaction, but there was nothing.

'I think he'd want me to send for the police,' she said, 'but he'll be here, soon, I can ask him.'

'Maybe he won't be here so soon as you think.'

That shook her. 'Why not?'

Mannering grinned, showing his discoloured teeth. He wasn't handsome in this guise, and had often practised that one-sided leer, worse in effect, he calculated, than the sardonic grin which had become a habit with Smith.

'He met with a little accident,' Mannering said.

Her eyes blazed, and she took a step forward; he thought she would come near enough for him to strike at the gun, but she kept just out of reach.

'*What do you mean?*'

'Just what I say, dearie,' Mannering said 'Smith thought he'd fixed me tonight, but I had a little surprise waiting for him. I'm good at surprises. He's had a nasty time, maybe he'll tell you all about it—when he wakes up. Of *if* he wakes up.' Voice, words and manner were all intended to unnerve her, and he noted with satisfaction that she had lost much of her poise. But the gun was steady, pointing unswervingly at his chest.

'What have you done to him?'

'Never you mind, dearie. Just put that gun down, and be sensible. Then you won't get hurt.'

'*I* won't get hurt.'

'That so? What about my pals, outside?'

Her head moved, upwards; but she stopped herself from looking round, robbing him of the chance of striking the gun aside. He needed only a split-second, but she wasn't easy to fool.

'There aren't any,' she said. 'I don't think you understand. If I shoot you, it'll be quite safe. I shall tell the police that I caught you in here, and you tried to attack me. Where is Paul?' She didn't seem to realise that she had said 'Paul', not Smith.

'Where would you expect him to be?' Mannering asked.

'Don't be clever. Remember that it will hurt if I shoot you.' She lowered the gun and now it covered his stomach. 'I'll aim where it hurts most.' The words took on even more sinister meaning coming so calmly, and in that pleasant voice. 'I mean what I say.'

'It would be your big mistake,' Mannering said.

He was only just out of reach of the gun. If the girl took one step nearer, he could knock it aside. But if he jumped she would shoot. Her forefinger was steady on the trigger, and he didn't like the expression in her eyes. It had been a mistake to tell her that he had injured her Paul. He felt the slow drops of sweat beading his forehead. He'd been in jams where the danger was more crude but none where it was greater. The beauty in her eyes was superseded by the smouldering hatred in them—outwardly, she was calm; inwardly she was afire, and it was the inward fire which might make her decide to shoot.

She said: 'If you don't tell me where Paul is, I shall shoot you in the guts.'

'Your insistence leaves me little choice. I left him at the garage. He was smart, but not quite so smart as he thought he was.'

'You couldn't have fooled *Paul*.' Fanatical belief in Smith was in her voice.

'Think so?' Feigning an ease he was far from feeling, Mannering sat down on the arm of a chair. It worked, as far as the fact that the girl visibly relaxed; but the gun stayed unmoving. 'Neither of you is so clever as you think you are, honey. You and your shadow!' He flung the word out again, but the reaction, or lack of it, was the same. It was obvious that she was thinking of Smith and the possibility that he was lying badly hurt. Mannering leaned back and grinned, and it wasn't a leer this time. 'You needn't worry,' he said. 'We had an argument, and I came out on the winning side, that's all. He's not hurt. We parted almost good friends, he thinks he might have a job for me, later on. He wasn't sure I was expert enough at breaking into places, and I thought I'd demonstrate. He won't argue about that in future.' Mannering actually laughed, and moved his hand towards his pocket.

'Keep your hands in sight,' she said. 'Paul wouldn't work with anyone else. You're lying.'

'All right, I'm lying. You don't have to believe me.' Mannering yawned. Suddenly, and for the first time, tension went out of her; the gun sagged, pointing at his feet.

He slid forward, propelling himself with his arms, and knocked against her with such force that the gun went off. He seized her arm and the weapon dropped to the floor. When he released her, she was limp and breathless. He pushed her off, snatched up the gun and slipped it into his own pocket, then moved away. She lay on the floor, still breathless but beginning to recover, her expression was baleful.

'Sorry I had to be rough,' said Mannering. 'I may have to be rougher. Remember I can put the cops on to your pal Paul any time I want to. If you kick up a shindy, you'll bring them in and I'll give Paul away.' He bent down and lifted her bodily. She struck him across the face, then drew back as his grip tightened. He carried her to the bathroom, stood her down, and went out, locking the door behind him.

He dragged a big settee across the door, then went back to the study. He examined the lock in the top of the desk, and tested it with a pick-lock. Short of shooting the lock, there was no other way to get at it. He might cut out a piece of the wood, but the top was probably steel-lined and he couldn't do anything about steel without an oxyacetylene cutter. If he were to break through here, he would have to use the pick-lock.

He went out to the front door, and left it wide open.

There was a risk that the older woman would turn up; he had to take that. But he had to make sure that he couldn't be caught unawares. He pushed the outer door to, and placed a chair across it so that it couldn't be moved without making a noise. Then he went into the kitchen. A fire escape led to a tiny back garden. Leaving that door open also, he returned to the desk and set to work with the pick-lock.

Five minutes convinced him that he hadn't a hope this way.

He went back to the kitchen, pulling open every drawer until he came to a small one, fitted out like a tool-chest; there was a chisel. He hesitated, and then opened a cupboard beneath the dresser. Then he laughed spontaneously, for there was an oxy-acetylene burner, a small cylinder and a pair of goggles.

The Shadow's equipment?

It was a light model, but still fairly weighty, and he grunted as he carried it to the study. There was no sound from the bathroom or from outside. He used a chisel on the unpolished wood, chipping it away round the key-hole. The noise was loud, but he hadn't time to be quiet. Soon, the bare steel round the key-hole lay revealed. He would have known after using the pick-lock if it was electrified, but he checked it carefully first, touching it lightly with the blade of his knife which had an insulated handle. There was no spark.

He hadn't used a cutter for a long time. . . .

He had been in the flat at least an hour and a half, but he forced himself to work carefully, and without panic. Through the dark goggles he saw the flame, cutting through the steel like a hot knife through butter. He cut out a square, then put the burner down, and prized the square out. After that, it was simply a matter of lifting back the top of the desk on its hinges.

It was empty; a big empty space, the shape of a coffin.

CHAPTER NINE

ALARM

He stood looking into the emptiness. If there were any valuables, or anything which Smith wanted to hide here, they would have been in the desk safe. There was nothing, he had wasted his time. He smiled wryly, feeling uneasy and frustrated. He could try to make the girl talk, but he didn't think she would be easily persuaded. He stood back and surveyed the ruin of the safe, picked up the chisel, and put it down again. He might as well get out, while the going was good.

But he couldn't assume that this was the only hiding place.

There might be others in the warehouse, or in one of the rooms; possibly in the flat across the landing.

He heard a clock strike twelve.

He moved into the hall. There was silence, everywhere. He walked across to the front door, paused to listen, heard nothing, and moved the chair aside. As he did so, he heard a creak. He stared tensely towards the door. It was open an inch, but he couldn't see the landing or the staircase, only a blank wall.

There was a shadow on the wall. It was not the shape of a man's head, but the shape of a policeman's helmet.

Another creaking sound came, but the shadow remained stationary; so someone else was there.

He put the chair back carefully, then moved silently across the room to the kitchen. He heard a sound, as if the door had been pushed against the chair. He could imagine the man outside trying to get an arm through so as to push the chair to one side. He stepped out into the cold night. Two or three lights showed at windows, and he could see the outline of the fire escape. It was impossible to go down without making some sound on the iron rungs.

He leaned forward, and held the rail and a faint clang came up to him.

He drew back, close against the wall, and waited. It was impossible to be sure how many men were on the fire escape. There were no sounds from inside the flat; the police were probably still trying to shift the chair without giving themselves away. He didn't move. He didn't ask himself what had brought the police. He felt his nerves quivering. He was sandwiched between two groups, and there would almost certainly be others, waiting below.

He saw the shape of a head appear on the landing then the head and shoulders of another. Pressed against the wall, he merged against the darkness. He held his breath as a man stepped into the kitchen. If the light were put on he would be seen.

The second man followed him; both were now inside the kitchen. Mannering heard them groping and saw the eerie beam of a torch light moving about. He stepped forward, groped for the first step, and started to go down. A policeman would probably be on guard, at the foot; he dare not make too much noise or lose too much time.

He reached the first landing, without raising an alarm. At the second, he could see the pale colour of the concrete in the back yard, and the dark shape of a policeman standing on it; the helmet was unmistakable. It was hard to believe that the man had neither seen or heard him. He went down the next few steps cautiously—and then the guard exclaimed:

'Here!'

Mannering said mildly: 'Hallo.'

The shadowy shape moved and Mannering jumped forward. The first shrill note of a whistle sounded. Next moment Mannering was on the man, smashing right and left at his stomach and face. The constable reeled back, and went sprawling. Mannering turned towards the dim shape of the wall; there was a lighter patch, where a door was open. He stepped through as the whistle shrilled out in earnest. He raced towards a street to which a narrow alley led. Another blast from the whistle cut the air, lights went up in several windows.

He heard pounding footsteps in close pursuit, and others coming towards him. Then the nearer man swung round the corner. Mannering shot out a foot and tripped him up, jumped past, and found himself near the steps which led to the lower level. The Buick was parked in the other direction. The headlights of two cars flared suddenly, and he was caught in a tunnel of light.

'There he is!' a man bellowed.

Mannering raced to the steps and leapt down, making for Villiers Street and the Underground Station. As unobtrusively as he could, he merged with several hurrying people, trying to breathe evenly, and behave as the average passenger obsessed with time. He forced himself to go at walking pace, reached the station and took a sixpenny ticket from the automatic machines. He was half way down the steps leading to the track before he heard a police whistle, so loud that he knew the police were in the station. A train came rumbling in. He reached the platform as it stopped, and stepped inside, then sat facing the platform. He saw two policemen hurrying down the steps as the train moved out, but the automatic closing doors were jammed tightly before they arrived.

They would be at the next station, Westminster, before the police could get there. He was at the doors before the train stopped, slipped out quickly, and hurried up to street level. He came out facing Big Ben, turned right, and reached the corner of Whitehall as a bus loomed up. He sprang onto the platform, clattered upstairs, then looked out of the window. He could see the people on the pavement, including two constables, but no one appeared to be in a hurry. He went as far as Victoria, changed buses, and booked to Marble Arch. By that time he felt safe, although the sight of a constable in uniform set his heart beating faster. For the first time, he had time to think; and he didn't want to think, that call had been too close. He went into the Cumberland Hotel, went to the main cloakroom, and shut himself into a W.C. He worked at his greasepaint with the rag and the little bottle of spirit. There was no mirror, he had to manage. He took the rubber off his teeth and the pads out of his cheeks, then he went out, took off his coat, and began to wash. Two other men were present, and neither noticed him.

The attendant came in, whistling off-key.

Mannering washed vigorously, and then examined himself in the mirror. There were traces of the grease paint, but not sufficient to give him away. Even an accurate description wouldn't help the police, but he'd feel happier when he was back at Chelsea, and out of these clothes.

He took a taxi to Victoria, then changed on to a bus; he couldn't cover his traces too thoroughly. From King's Road he walked briskly towards River Walk. A cold wind was blowing off the Thames, invigorating and welcome. Now that the crisis was past, he could begin to examine it. Why the police had decided to raid Buckley Street.

Had they been watching the house, and seen what had happened earlier?

He didn't think that was the answer, or they would have acted sooner.

It was more likely that the shot had been heard, or that a patrol constable had found the door forced, and sent for a raiding party. The cause didn't greatly matter, and there was little risk of being discovered. No one that night had seen him as he really was, no one would recognise him if they saw him now. Yet he was uneasy.

As he neared the house, he saw a man in a doorway on the other side of the road.

It was a favourite point of vantage, for those who thought it worth watching him; Bristow's men particularly. He fought down a flare of alarm. Although he could be heard, he couldn't be seen definitely enough to be recognised. He walked past the doorway of his house, towards the Embankment. He stopped at the first corner, and glanced round; there was no sign of the watching man. He waited for a few minutes, and the man didn't emerge from his hiding place. The sense of acute danger faded. Mannering made his way towards the back of the house. It was an easy climb up to a window of his flat; he'd made it easy, with iron brackets, because in the past he'd often found it useful.

Hetty, the maid, was probably asleep; in any case, there was no light in her room. He climbed cautiously through the window, but didn't breathe really freely until he reached his own bedroom.

Then he began to laugh. It was crazy laughter, and he couldn't stop himself. As he took off the clothes and hung them up at the back of the wardrobe, he was still chuckling. He went to the bathroom and ran the bath water hot, finishing off with a cold shower. He didn't go to bed, but switched on the electric fire in the study, and sat looking into it. Every now and again, he chuckled again. After a while, he poured himself out a strong whisky and soda, and it was then that he saw the telephone note propped on an ashtray. He read:

'10 o'clock . . . .Mr. Plender, no message.
10.45 . . . . .Mr. Plender, no message.
11.30 . . . . .A man rang up but wouldn't give his name.
12.20 . . . . .A man rang up, the same one I think, and wouldn't give his name.'

He took a deep drink, and carried glass and slip of paper to the chair. He frowned as he read it again. Who was the mysterious caller? And why had Toby tried to get him twice on the same evening? There was probably a simple explanation of Toby Plender's call, there was no reason why he shouldn't try again if he were unlucky the first time; but who had the anonymous caller been?

He began to build menace into those last two calls. Who would want to speak to him at twenty past twelve?

There was no telling whether anyone else had called up later, or whether the same man had tried to ring him again. Hetty had probably dropped off to sleep quickly, and she was a heavy sleeper. The telephone bell was some distance from her bedroom.

He looked at the telephone. There was an extension in the hall, another in the drawing-room. He frowned towards it, as if willing it to ring, or to tell him how many times in the past hour and a half, it had been ringing without getting a response.

He finished his whisky, and put the glass down.

Then the telephone rang.

* * *

He stood up, slowly, torn between the temptation to let it go on ringing, and the desire to know who was calling him. He glanced at his watch; it was now nearly two fifteen. The ringing went on, persistent and regular. He reached the telephone, and lifted the receiver slowly. He yawned, near the mouthpiece, and spoke in a voice which seemed heavy with sleep.

'Hallo? Who's that?'
'Is that Mr. Mannering?'
'Yes.' He yawned again. 'Who—'
The caller rang off.

*   *   *

The worst of the mysterious telephone call was that he didn't understand the reason for it. He stood watching the instrument, as if it would wake to life again; and then turned abruptly to the window. Switching the light off, he pulled the curtains aside, and stared into the street. He could see the doorway where the man had been hiding, but could not see the man. Fighting down a growing lassitude, he continued to stand there, and at last he was rewarded. A car appeared, its headlights pinpointing for less than a second the man who had been watching. The car slowed and stopped, the headlights went out. Everything seemed pitch dark after that, but when the effect of the glare had gone, he saw two men talking. A third joined them; a policeman in uniform.

There was nothing more to learn, he might as well go to bed. But his lassitude had been blasted away.

It was obvious that the police had been checking, to find out whether he had been in during the evening and now knew that he hadn't. The watcher would be able to say that he had not returned by the front door, so the police would know he had returned by the back way; and risked the wall climb.

They would want to know why.

He knew that Chief Inspector Gordon was constantly on the alert, hoping to catch him out; that with the activities of the Shadow, there was bound to be a revival of interest in the Baron. Here, in the darkness of the small hours, it was easy to believe that Bristow would misconstrue his reason for refusing to help 'catch' the Shadow; that the police were building up a strong case against him; that they knew he had been out tonight; that they knew he had been at Buckley Street, which explained the reason for their raid. The police had hoped to catch him red-handed.

They'd rung up, at intervals, and knew what time he had been out.

They would probably let him settle down, thinking that there would be no further scare tonight, and then they would call.

To have all his wits about him he must stay awake. It would be foolish even to doze. He didn't feel like smoking or reading; but gradually, too slowly to cause alarm, tiredness crept over him. He heard three o'clock strike.

He couldn't keep his eyes open.

He went to sleep.

CHAPTER TEN

NEWS

He heard voices, and one of them was a man's.

He woke on the instant, listening intently; a woman was talking. It was Hetty, and she was complaining and excusing herself at the same time. She couldn't take upon herself to wake Mr. Mannering. She'd already been in with his tea and he hadn't stirred, she might lose her job if she woke him. Actually she knew she wouldn't lose it, which meant that she had a strong reason for not wanting him to be disturbed; or that was what he assumed. He pushed the bedclothes back. After the first shock of sudden waking, he felt clear-headed. The bedside clock showed that it was a little after nine.

As he climbed out of bed and put on his dressing-gown, he heard the man say 'Hetty, I *must* see him, I tell you.' He recognised the voice as Larraby's.

Mannering grinned and relaxed, and opened the door wide. They didn't notice him when he stepped into the hall. Hetty, big and cumbersome, a country girl thoroughly enjoying a strict sense of duty, was barring Larraby's path.

'Hetty, you're fired,' said Mannering.

Hetty jumped and turned round, her mouth opening in astonishment.

'Unless you make me some tea right away,' added Mannering.

'Oh, I *will*, sir. Mr. Larraby shouldn't have disturbed you, I'm ever so sorry, I did try to make him keep his voice down.' She glared at Larraby with the self-righteousness of a conscientious servant who knew her worth, and was determined that others should know it also.

'Come in, Josh,' Mannering said. 'What's up?'

'Is everything all right, sir?'

'Why shouldn't it be?'

'I was nervous,' said Larraby. His habitually serene expression was tinged with anxiety as he took a bundle of newspapers from under his arm. 'You haven't seen these, have you?' He held them out. 'I felt that I had to come and tell you what *might* happen this morning.'

Mannering didn't glance at the papers.

'All right, Josh—but first, what happened last night?'

'I was there for over an hour, and then a man came up and let them out,' said Josh. 'I couldn't see him clearly, but it was a young chap. Well dressed, too. They talked for a bit, and then Smith went off in a taxi. The other two stayed at the garage. I was tempted to follow Smith, but even if I'd wanted to I hadn't another cab. I kept away from Buckley Street—I hope that was right, Mr. Mannering.'

'More right than you know,' said Mannering.

He unfolded the top paper. The headline seemed to leap out at him:

SHADOW STRIKES AGAIN
£20,000 MAYFAIR HAUL

The Shadow, notorious jewel-thief, struck again in the early hours of the morning, and escaped with £20,000 worth of jewels from the Morley Square home of Sir James Leeson. The theft. . . .

'Are they all the same, Josh?'

'Very much the same. But there is another thing, sir. I heard a rumour this morning that the police know who the Shadow is, and hope to make an arrest soon. I also heard that there had been a burglary at Buckley Street. I assumed that you went to Buckley Street again, and—' Larraby broke off, and gave a little, hesitant smile. 'I'm a little confused, but I was very anxious you should be informed about the rumour that the police have a line on the man at last.'

'Very sensible of you,' Mannering said. 'Have you had breakfast, Josh?'

'Well—'

'Go and make peace with Hetty over bacon and eggs,' Mannering said. 'Then slip out, and stay away until I send for you. Have you decided where to stay yet?'

'At the Grayville—a small place in Dover street, sir. I know the management and can have a room with a telephone.'

Alone again, Mannering drank hot tea and smoked a cigarette, keeping an ear cocked for the front door bell. It didn't ring. He shaved and bathed, and had breakfast, and it was half past ten before he had finished. By then, Larraby had gone.

The telephone bell rang, suddenly.

Mannering lifted the receiver warily. 'John Mannering speaking.'

'Hold on, please, I've a call from Salisbury for you.'

Salisbury meant Lorna. He leaned back, beaming.

'Darling.' Lorna's voice was faint.

'I've been waiting for the past hour for this,' said Mannering, with reproach that became genuine the moment he had voiced it.

'Darling, are you all right?'

'Of course I'm all right.'

'Why aren't you at the shop?'

'I woke up too late.'

'John, have you seen the newspapers?'

'I have, indeed.'

'John, were you out late last night?'

'Not so late apparently as the Shadow.'

There was a pause, and then Lorna said in a more definite voice:

'I wish I knew whether to believe you or not.'

'It's not worth the effort, my dear, believe me in that. How's your mother?'

'Not too good,' Lorna said, 'I can't leave her, otherwise, of course, I'd be in London with you. I don't trust you on your own. John, be careful. Don't take any risks.'

'I'm growing older and wiser,' Mannering said.

'Older, certainly. Telephone me sometime tonight.'

'I will,' promised Mannering. 'And if you think I ought to come to Salisbury—'

'I would like you to, though I can't pretend

it's a matter of life and death,' Lorna said. 'Just be careful.'

She rang off, abruptly. Mannering replaced the receiver, seeing his wife in his mind's eye. He sat back for ten minutes, with the same thoughtful expression on his face, then picked up the newspapers, and read them thoroughly for the first time. He scanned them for the slightest detail that might help, then threw them aside. He felt restless, anxious to know what had transpired at Buckley Street, in one way glad that the desk-safe had been empty. If the police had found a haul there, Smith and the girl would by now be lodged at the police station. The papers said nothing about an arrest.

Why hadn't he heard from Bristow?

Could he have been wrong about the identity of the man who had been watching the flat?

He would have assumed that he had, but for the memory of the uniformed figure who had joined the other two. Bristow knew he had been out; Bristow was probably certain that he was the burglar of Buckley Street. Mannering checked over all that had happened and what he had said to the girl; he could find no weak link. He'd left no prints, nothing with which he could be identified.

Bristow would be furious, the constables he had bowled over would probably be even more so, but there was nothing the police could do.

Bristow wasn't likely to ask for his help again in a hurry.

Then the front door bell rang.

He listened, as Hetty plodded heavily across the hall. Her words were indistinct. But he recognised the voice of the man who spoke; it was Bristow.

* * *

Bristow came in, smiling broadly. He crossed the study and shook hands. The gardenia in his buttonhole was fresh, his suit was newly pressed, he seemed to be at peace with the world; this wasn't the harassed and mortified policeman Mannering had pictured in his mind's eye.

'Hallo, John. Feeling off colour?'

'I'm fine,' said Mannering cautiously.

'If tactlessness might be forgiven an old friend, you certainly don't look it,' said Bristow. 'Thanks.' He lit a cigarette and sat down carefully adjusting the crease of his trousers. 'So you had a lie-in this morning.'

'Time being my own,' Mannering said. The

years had taught him to beware of an affable Bristow.

'Lucky beggar, I wish I could suit myself as you do. Where did you go last night? The *Lulu*.'

'Why the *Lulu*?'

'I have my spies in unexpected places!'

'Including my doorstep,' Mannering said, smiling dryly. 'He had a shock last night, didn't he?'

'Eh?'

'Such innocence, Bill!' said Mannering. 'He didn't see me come in, and was shaken when he discovered I was, in fact, in the flat.'

'Must be a Divisional job,' said Bristow, 'I didn't know anything about it. Did you dodge him?'

'No point in losing one's touch,' Mannering said airily.

'How did you get in?'

'What an insatiable appetite the police have for detail! The significant point is, that I was awakened by a mysterious voice on the telephone.'

'Now I wonder whose that could have been,' said Bristow. 'I'll have to find out! Didn't you have a chat with Toby Plender recently?'

Mannering raised his eyebrows.

'John, I wish I'd come to you myself, instead of approaching you through Plender. I should have known you'd guess who prompted him. There's a lot you could do to help.'

'How?' asked Mannering.

'I can't go into that unless you decide to help,' said Bristow. 'That's reasonable, isn't it? And if you think that I've a notion that the Baron and the Shadow are one and the same man, forget it. Some people may think so, but I know better. You know he was about again last night, I suppose.'

'The newspapers conveyed that much to me,' murmured Mannering.

'He's probably going to be a thorn in our flesh for a long time to come.' Bristow's frankness was disarming, but behind it was a keen and probing mind. He was convinced that Mannering had been out the previous night, had made sure Mannering realised that he knew. 'You know, I think this is the work of more than one man, the method of approach being identical. It's only a guess, and I don't use it officially, but I've a feeling that I'm not far wrong. John, you've channels of information we can't get at. Have you heard of any of the Shadow's stuff being on the market anywhere?'

'Nowhere, Bill.'

'Pity. Has it occurred to you that he might be unloading the stuff across the Channel?'

'I haven't thought much about it,' Mannering said.

'Well, it's time you did! But I mustn't stay, I've a lot to do.' Bristow rose slowly from his chair. 'Seriously, John, if you feel you can help us against the Shadow, we'd jump at the chance. It isn't a normal job. Anderson-Kerr is quite amenable. Great Scott, look at the time!' He shook hands again, brisk and breezy, not waiting for Mannering to open either door. 'I'll look forward to hearing from you,' he said, and bustled down the stairs.

Mannering closed the door behind him, smoothed down his hair, and began to whistle. He went back into the study and watched from the window. He saw Bristow's green Morris parked outside, the Yard man climb in. Looking across the road, he saw that a man was still on duty in the doorway of the empty house, making no attempt, by day, to conceal himself. The man saluted as the car moved off; evidence that he was a Yard man and that Bristow knew he was there. Bristow's breeziness wasn't worth a moment's serious thought. Bristow had come to confuse and bewilder him; a kind of warning off. Could Bristow be thinking that the Shadow was the Baron?

CHAPTER ELEVEN

OFF THE RECORD

Mannering spent half an hour at Quinns, then drove to Fleet Street, parked his car near Ludgate Circus and walked to the Red Lion public house. It was approached from a narrow side street and beneath a wide arch, where once carriages and post-chaises had rattled over the cobbles and lamp-boys had sprung to attention as the guests arrived. The Red Lion remained an attractive building, with bottle-glass windows, and a litchened roof, its door always open to receive guests. There were few casual callers, most who visited it were habitués; and most of the habitués had some connection with Fleet Street.

A blast of hot air from an open fireplace greeted Mannering as he entered. He nodded amiably to the two or three men sitting around and went into the main bar. It was early, but the bar was crowded.

A few men glanced at the newcomer, one of them called: 'Come and join us, Mannering.'

'I wish I could,' said Mannering.

He caught sight of a small curly-haired man standing in a corner, with a pint tankard in his hand. Bright blue eyes flickered over Mannering. A hint of a smile followed.

Mannering joined him.

The curly-haired man lifted a tankard from a tray which was being carried past him, and offered it.

'Thirsty?'

'Thanks. Got a story for me, John?'

'Afraid not, I'm merely a grass-widower with time on his hands. How is Chittering of the *Record* these days?'

The expression in the blue eyes was one of utmost candour. 'Put me down as a hard chap to convince, but I don't believe in the innocence of grass-widowers. I suspect that the great J.M. is thirsty for information and will drink beer with the lowly in order to get what he wants. Will you have a bite with me?'

'Thanks.'

'Suspicions confirmed,' said Chittering. 'I have a telephone call to make and a quiet corner to reserve. I'll be seeing you.' He wandered off, tankard in hand, and others surged upon Mannering. There had been a rumour that Quinns had been robbed, was it true? If so, Mannering had been damned close about it. The rumour, it transpired, had started from a nightclub, known as *Lulu's*. Mannering was bland; it had been a false alarm.

'Haven't you some Heath Robinson burglar proof contraptions?' asked a large man with a bald head.

'Nothing is burglar proof.'

'Can I quote you?'

'Certainly.'

'Tied up with the Shadow?'

'Will nothing I say convince you?' cried Mannering in mock despair.

Chittering passing through the crowded room like a wraith, led the way up the narrow, twisted stairs to the smallest of three dining-rooms. The head waiter greeted Mannering warmly. The wine was already on the table.

They ordered with due care.

'Now what?' asked Chittering, settling back in his chair. 'You needn't say it, everything's off the record at the moment. The Shadow?'

'What makes you think so?'

'Your pal Plender,' said Chittering. 'I hear rumours. Rumour one—the great J.M. and his beautiful wife were at the *Lulu* Club with the distinguished T.B., Q.C., and his vivacious wife. Rumour two—J.M. is called out to an emergency, at Quinns. Rumour three—

Mrs. Plender is sorrowing over the loss of a family heirloom. Known fact—the heirloom gets back. Rumour—J.M. brought influence to bear upon the Shadow.'

Mannering looked alarmed.

'How far has that rumour spread?'

'I've just started it.'

'You're a public danger,' Mannering said.

'Oh, no. Just a danger to famous jewel collectors who masquerade as shopkeepers,' said Chittering. 'Ah!' There were oysters. 'What's it all about, John?' he asked, as the last of a dozen finished its journey.

'There was a raid on a house in the Adelphi last night,' said Mannering.

'How do you get to know things! It didn't reach the Street until half-past eleven, I doubt if it was published until after you got here. A damp squib, though. There was a shot or two fired at a flat in Buckley Street. Hardly a story, except that a bee-ootiful damsel fired it in defence, she says, of her honour. As she was locked in the bathroom, there is some doubt about that. A wideawake constable heard the fireworks, and called for help. He had already discovered that the downstairs lock had been forced. But the forcer fooled the police. The Yard and the Division concerned are sore about it, though nothing was stolen. The girl was alone in the flat, and says that she disturbed a burglar, fired, but didn't hit him. That's the story. Why are you interested?'

'That girl brought joy to Mrs. Plender's life,' Mannering said.

Chittering looked interested. 'Fact?'

'Off the record, as we said.'

'Yes, of course. You get around, John. So you were on the spot when the pendant was returned. It happened the night of the rumoured raid on Quinns. I'm beginning to see. Well, the police didn't find anything at Buckley Street. I was round at the Back Room myself this morning, and have had a chat with Gordon and one or two of the others. The tenant of the flat—'

'Tenant?'

'All right, all right, the man who owns the whole house,' said Chittering. 'Name of Smith. Quite a personality. He doesn't look at all like a man who runs a mail order business. It's a crime to run one of those from the historic Adelphi, but you know what modern businessmen are like. Where was I?'

The steak arrived with much garnishing.

'You had reached the stage where he came on the scene.'

'Oh, yes. He was out until half-past one. By then, the police were in possession, and the girl had been released. There was a desk safe, empty. Smith said it had been empty for some time, and that nothing was lost. The police did a good job of searching and turned the warehouse upside down, but nothing appears to have been taken away. An elderly woman, who was out during the night, turned up this morning and was all of a flutter when she discovered what had happened. She is an aunt.'

'Mr. Smith's aunt?'

'The lovely's. Aunt-cum-chaperone-cum-housekeeper, I understand. I suppose you want to know the girl's name?'

'Thanks.'

'Celia.'

'Smith?'

'Fleming. Background—mysterious.'

'You seem to have been delving to some purpose,' said Mannering.

Chittering chuckled.

'Why not? You know my Editor—get the feminine allure angle, and let the rest go hang. As a matter of fact, I spent ten minutes with her this morning. She didn't say much, and Smith was present. When I asked an awkward question he made some remark which saved her face. The fact is, of course, they're living together in every sense of the word. The aunt is simply a blind. I'll tell you what,

John.'

'Well, what?'

'I wouldn't like to be the man who tried to do harm to Paul Smith. Every now and again you come across what romantics once called the supreme passion. Celia has it for Paul. She worships him.' Chittering paused for a few minutes, and then went on thoughtfully: 'Amazing.'

'Why?'

'Difficult to say. Celia is a typical modern product—the factory-made type of the moment that scorns all but ephemeral relationships and emotions, and yet—' he paused again. 'The incongruity shook me. I just didn't like it. I had the impression that he exerts what might be called an influence over her. The Svengali touch.' He toyed with his steak for a moment, then he looked frankly into Mannering's eyes.

'John, I'm not particularly impressionable. Life is life and I could tell you a lot about its seamy side. The fact is, there's a quality in Celia Fleming that got under my skin. Her whole personality has been withdrawn or subdued under the weight of another. It is as if Paul Smith had taken complete possession of her, of her mind and her thoughts as well as her heart and body. Tell me I'm mad.'

Mannering said slowly: 'And Smith?'

'Bad,' said Chittering.

'Had you ever heard of him before?'

'No. I don't think I want to, again. I should not like to get on his wrong side. Think he's the Shadow?' Chittering put the question almost casually, and when Mannering didn't answer, elaborated. 'I think you're after the Shadow and there's a man who could be up to all the tricks.'

'I'm just probing, so far,' Mannering said. 'It was Celia who took the pendant back to Plender.'

'That makes her the Shadow's messenger.'

'It could do.'

'What's going on in that thing you call a mind?'

'Confusion,' Mannering said, and smiled amiably.

'I'm not surprised. Does Bristow know who brought the pendant back?'

'No. Nor does Plender.'

'Just a little secret between us two,' said Chittering. 'All right, John, I won't give anything away. Are you seriously after the Shadow?'

'Not yet. I'm rather attached to him.'

'If he's Paul Smith, get unattached.'

'That,' said Mannering cryptically, 'is

what I mean. What about the Shadow, by the way? You've probably got more information about him than I have.'

'There isn't much we haven't used,' said Chittering. 'A courteous, gallant thief, if there be such a thing these days. He hasn't hurt a hair of anybody's head. Two or three times he might have got away with much more stuff than he did, if he'd biffed someone. He preferred not to biff. That may simply be build-up. On the other hand, any fool knows that if he's caught and has a record of violence, he'll get a longer sentence than if he just lifts the stuff. It probably isn't romantic at all, merely calculated common sense. Paul Smith would have that kind.'

'Hmm,' said Mannering.

'When this story breaks, from your end, I want it first,' said Chittering.

'It'll be yours. But you'll probably have to work for it.'

'How?'

'Try to find out more about the girl's background, will you? Where she comes from, whether she has a family, all that kind of thing.'

'I can't see why, unless you've taken on the championship of fallen angels.'

'Could be the outward and visible sign of a

reformed character.'

Chittering almost spluttered over his coffee.

* * *

There followed two unexpectedly quiet days. The police continued to watch Mannering's flat; Lorna remained at Salisbury and was likely to stay there for another week. Plender, it proved, had telephoned simply to inquire after Lady Fauntley, Lorna's mother. Larraby made many underground inquiries, but discovered nothing of interest. Mannering did not hear from Chittering during those two days, and spent much of the time with the cleaned picture, which two experts said was Rubens and two said was a good imitation.

Early on the evening of the second day, Chittering telephoned.

'Hallo, John. Tired?'

'Not yet,' said Mannering.

'That's good. Don't ask me why, but put on your best bib and tucker and join me at *Lulu's* at ten o'clock. O.K.?'

'O.K.,' said Mannering.

CHAPTER TWELVE

PRESENT FROM CHITTERING

Chittering looked more boyish than ever in tails. He introduced his sister Jane, a buxom girl whom Mannering instantly associated with hockey sticks and basket ball, and Chloe, tall, whippet thin and unsmiling.

She looked at Mannering out of sleepy eyes.

Chittering beamed.

He ordered champagne with the air of one saluting an occasion. Alone with Mannering for a moment he drew his attention to the fact that a table for two had been reserved. 'The one over there, in the corner.'

Mannering said: 'Paul and Celia?'

'Of course. There is also someone else present,' said Chittering. 'See the distinguished johnny with the sky-blue wife? Near the door.'

Mannering had noticed the couple.

'Just watch,' said Chittering, 'and I'll unburden myself later.'

Mannering shrugged, aware of a slow, expectant stir among the crowd. Now, Paul

Smith and Celia Fleming entered—and heads turned appreciatively towards them.

Celia wore dark red and she looked superb; yet it was the man who caught the attention. He came in as if he were owed homage, surveying those in the room as a Roman Emperor might have surveyed his gladiators. His gaze, passing over Mannering, rested for a moment on Chittering, and his smile widened sardonically. Not a pretty woman was passed over by that all-seeing eye; several turned their heads away abruptly.

Mannering toying with a glass, watched Smith without appearing to do so.

He saw that sweeping gaze suddenly arrested, the smile vanished. The man's expression became hard, his eyes glittered; he looked as if he had seen someone whom he hated. Then he took Celia's arm, and led her to the table in the corner. Lulu fussed after them.

The change had come when Smith had looked at the couple described by Chittering as 'the distinguished johnny with the sky-blue wife.'

Mannering shifted his chair, so that he could see them better. The man, probably in the early forties, was handsome in a formal way. He had an air of well-being, and there was nothing in his expression to suggest that he was aware of Smith's attention. The woman looked motherly and harassed; it was easy to tell that it was she who had been disturbed by that raking glance.

'Who?' asked Mannering.

'Major, courtesy title only, Fleming. And Mrs. Fleming. They have one daughter.'

Mannering said: 'Well, well!'

'I couldn't resist springing it on you,' Chittering said. 'I knew that Smith often came here, and kept an eye on the advance bookings. Lulu's always helpful. Then I discovered that some Flemings had also booked for tonight, so I did a bit of detective work, and discovered that they have a daughter Celia. She left home nearly a year ago. They live in Guildford—he's semi-retired, does a bit of fruit farming and keeps livestock of one kind or another. Oh—Oxford, the old type. You can tell that at a glance.'

Mannering said: 'Here's Chloe.'

They danced. Mannering discovered that though she remained as silent and dreamy-eyed as ever, Chloe danced extremely well. Rather surprisingly, he enjoyed it.

Smith and Celia Fleming rose at once, melting into the dance just that little bit better than any other couple on the floor. The Flemings watched from their table, until the tempo increased and several couples dropped out. Mannering and Chloe, Smith and Celia and three other couples were alone on the floor.

Then Fleming got up.

His wife put out a hand, as if to stop him. Fleming smiled at her, and walked towards the dance floor.

Turning, Smith saw him, and missed a step.

Fleming smiled; but it wasn't a normal smile, and Mannering seeing his hands clenched, half expected what was coming. If Smith guessed, he did nothing about it. Suddenly, without fuss or bother Fleming hit him.

'*Oh!*' gasped Chloe, and fell against Mannering.

Smith bent double, hands at his stomach, Fleming hit him again. At that tense moment, the band stopped, hypnotised by what was happening on the floor. Smith staggered and then fell. Fleming turned away, as if at an unpleasant job completed. It was then that Celia leapt at him. There was fury in her eyes, as she beat at his face with clawed fingers. Fleming backed away, trying to fend her off, it was like trying to keep away from a tiger.

Smith began to pick himself up.

Mannering reached Celia, and gripped her round the waist. Every muscle in her body was quivering, he could see her teeth clenched beneath her drawn lips. Fleming, with blood on his cheeks and one eye closed, moved back to his wife who was standing like a statue, by her table.

Celia stood in Mannering's grasp, glaring at the man whom he believed to be her father. The hatred smouldered and flared up again in her eyes. Indifferent to Mannering, she made no attempt to get away.

Smith put a hand on Mannering's arm.

'Enough,' he said.

Mannering let the girl go. Smith took her back to the table. She sat down, looking straight ahead of her. Mannering watched her with concealed interest. She was rigid, head in a statuesque and unnatural calm. Without speaking, Smith refilled her glass. He put something into her hand, and she took it automatically. A moment later, she put her hand to her mouth, and then sipped champagne. After that, she closed her eyes and sat quite still.

The Flemings were already out of the room.

Mannering returned to his table as the band struck up. Chloe was looking excited,

Jane stunned. Chittering's expression held the cherubic false innocence of a fourteen-year-old.

'Chloe,' said Mannering, 'you'll never forgive me, but I have to go. I'd forgotten that I had an appointment. If I can get back, I will. If not, another night—you're the most accomplished dancer I know.' He took her hand and bowed low over it, smiled towards the silent Jane, and hurried to the door.

On the first floor, by the cloakroom, Lulu was murmuring to Major Fleming that she was sure he quite understood that she would rather he never came to the club again. Fleming was dabbing at his eye with a blood-stained handkerchief, and a girl was helping his wife into her coat. Mannering hurried downstairs ahead of them, and was waiting on the pavement when they arrived.

The commissionaire said: 'Cab, sir?'

'Oh, *please*,' cried Mrs. Fleming.

'I wonder if I can help, my car's handy,' said Mannering.

'Well, I—' began Mrs. Fleming.

Fleming said: 'Thank you, Mr. Mannering.'

'You know each other?' Mrs. Fleming sounded surprised and relieved. Neither of the men spoke again, and soon they were in the

Sunbeam Talbot.

'Where to?' Mannering asked.

'The Milne Court Hotel,' said Fleming, mentioning a small and exclusive hotel in Knightsbridge.

Mannering drove fast, and they reached the hotel just before one o'clock.

'Come and have a drink, Mannering,' said Fleming.

'Bob, you really ought to have your face—'

'Thanks,' said Mannering. 'I'm useful at first-aid Mrs. Fleming.'

They passed the night staff, ignoring their discreet surprise at Fleming's cut face. Reaching their room, Fleming unlocked the door, and stood aside. Mrs. Fleming led the way in, Mannering followed. He saw her shrink back, could imagine the scream which sprang to her lips. He leapt to her support as Fleming exclaimed:

'What's the matter? What—'

Then his voice trailed off.

A girl lay on the bed, with her arms outflung, one leg hanging over the side. A stocking was tied tightly round her neck. Her lips were parted, her eyes half open and glazed.

CHAPTER THIRTEEN

MURDER

Mrs. Fleming slumped down, a dead weight. Mannering half carried her to a chair, and eased her into it. He stood back as Fleming closed the door and walked across to the bed. He stood looking down, for the moment stunned, incapable of taking any further action. Mannering pushed past him, taking a penknife from his pocket. The stocking was buried into the girl's neck, and the knot was too tight for him to undo. He eased the blade between the skin and the stocking, and began to cut. Strands fell apart.

'It's a waste of time,' Fleming said harshly.

Mannering felt the girl's pulse. Fleming was right; there was no trace of movement.

Mrs Fleming began to moan.

Fleming said: 'So he's got me.'

'Smith?'

'Yes. He swore that he would finish me.' Fleming's voice was strangely quiet.

'So you know the girl?'

'Yes. She's a friend of Celia, my daughter.'

'Her name.'

'Muriel Lee.'

'A friend of yours, too?'

'No. I always blamed her for what happened to Celia.'

'Starting her on dope, you mean?'

'Yes.'

'Had you quarrelled?'

'The last time I saw the girl, I told her that I'd gladly kill her. That was in public.'

'Pity,' said Mannering. 'And you seriously think that Smith lured the girl here, and killed her?'

'Or had her killed.'

'The story might stand up,' said Mannering. 'Murder's hard to pin on to an innocent man. The police aren't fools. Any reason to think you could get evidence against Smith?'

'None whatever.'

'In that case,' Mannering said crisply, 'you can do one of three things. Send for the police immediately. Run away and hide—'

'Not that,' Fleming said. 'That's what Smith probably thinks I'll do.'

Mannering didn't comment on that strange remark, but finished imperturbably, 'Or we could get the girl out of here.'

Fleming said: 'Don't be a fool, Mannering.' He went across to the bedside telephone.

'Don't call the police yet,' Mannering said.

'I'd like you to tell me first what the position is. Celia is your daughter. Paul Smith has taken her away from her family. There's hatred between you. What started it?'

'He hypnotised her—fascinated her—call it what you like. She changed completely. She was a lovely girl, kind and good. He turned her whole character. You saw what happened tonight. She worships him. He keeps her mind dulled through drugs. She hasn't got to the stage where she can be—helped—in the usual way. Fleming passed a shaking hand over his face. 'I've known Smith for some time. God forgive me, it was through me they met.'

'Where did you meet him?'

'In the Army.'

'Will you tell me why you decided to go to *Lulu's* tonight?'

'There's one way to hurt Smith—through his pride. Being humiliated in public would hurt him more than anything I know. I went there just to do that.'

'Well, you did it,' Mannering said.

Mrs. Fleming's eyes were flickering and she was making little moaning sounds. Fleming went across to her, and knelt by the side of the chair, taking her hands.

'Call the police for me, Mannering, will

you.'

Mannering dialled Whitehall 1212. He was hardly surprised to hear that Bristow wasn't in his office. He spoke to an Inspector, rang off and dialled another number.

Bristow's voice answered, sharp and clear.

'Hallo, John. Going to make a confession?'

'Yes. I butted in where I needn't have done, and found a corpse. It's nothing to do with me, Bill, but it's on your beat. The Milne Court Hotel, Knightsbridge, and yes, I'll be waiting here.' He rang off before Bristow could comment, and sauntered across to the Flemings.

'I can't stand it any longer, I can't stand it,' Mrs. Fleming muttered. She began to shiver.

'We've got to get her out of here,' Fleming said urgently.

'That shouldn't take long.' Mannering looked hard into the woman's face and then went back to the telephone. After some hesitation he was put through to the manager. 'Will you come along to Room 55, with some brandy?' asked Mannering. 'This is urgent. I would also like to know if there is a vacant room nearby?'

'Who is that speaking?'

'I'm speaking for Major Fleming—there's been an accident.'

'Expect me in one minute.' The manager's voice was tense. Mannering replaced the receiver and watched Fleming, who now stood hopelessly by his wife's side. She had closed her eyes again; she seemed to have aged ten years in the past hour.

Mannering said: 'Why did you ask me to come upstairs, Fleming?'

'Oh, never mind now.'

'It matters.'

Fleming passed a hand over his hair.

'I know you by reputation. When you interfered tonight, I thought you might be interested in Paul Smith. I hoped you'd have something to tell me about him.'

There was a tap at the door.

Outside, a small dapper man was standing with a bottle of brandy and two glasses, on a tray.

'As it was urgent, I brought it myself. I'm the manager, Major Fleming—'

He looked past Mannering and saw the girl on the bed; as the tray tilted, Mannering put a hand beneath it. One glass fell heavily to the carpeted floor.

'Where's that vacant room?' asked Mannering.

* * *

A police patrol car arrived first, and the men reached the second floor as Mrs. Fleming was being taken into a room three doors away. Hard on their heels, two men arrived from Scotland Yard, and before they had started to ask questions, Bristow himself arrived. Three other Yard men and a police surgeon followed, and the large room was crowded. Bristow took charge, and seemed satisfied to take Mannering's word for what had happened. Cameramen got busy, finger print men started to search for their clues. The police went about their work quickly, calmly and with impressive thoroughness. Bristow seemed unaware that Fleming and Mannering were still in the room but he had sent a man to stand outside Mrs. Fleming's door. A maid was with her.

Bristow crossed to Mannering and Fleming.

'You all arrived together?'

'Yes, Bill.'

'Who saw the body first?'

'My wife,' said Fleming.

'And then?'

'Mr. Mannering.'

'Who cut the stocking away?'

'I did,' Mannering said.

'Hmm. Mr. Fleming, I'd like to see you

alone for a few minutes—the manager will let us have the use of a room. Have you sent for a doctor to see your wife?'

Fleming said: 'All she needs is rest.'

'She ought to see a doctor. I'll get Dr. Mortimer to look at her.' Bristow went across to the police surgeon, who was finishing a cursory examination of the body, and the three men left the room together.

Bristow was gone a long time; he came back alone.

'Well, John!'

'My turn,' murmured Mannering.

'So far, so good,' said Bristow, smiling. 'I've already checked that you reached the *Lulu* Club just before ten o'clock and didn't leave until you came straight here. I also know that this room was empty at five minutes past ten, when a maid came in to put hot water bottles in the bed. So that lets you out!'

'And the Flemings?'

'Did you think they were surprised?'

'They looked surprised all right. I can't see into their minds,' Mannering said.

'What did Fleming tell you?'

'It'll only be hearsay.'

'It will help me check on what he's told me,' said Bristow. 'You'll probably find it out yourself, so there's no reason why I shouldn't tell you. The Flemings came back to the hotel at a quarter past ten, and left twenty minutes later. Mrs. Fleming was agitated. You see what that could mean?'

'Yes, I see,' said Mannering, and repeated what Fleming had told him. The telling took five minutes; relating all that had happened at the *Lulu* Club took another ten. By that time, the preliminary work of the police was done, the finger print men were packing up their equipment and the photographers were already on their way to the Yard. A sheet had been drawn over the girl's face.

'It's a peculiar business,' Bristow said. 'This daughter, Celia, really went for her father, did she?'

'Like a wildcat.'

'How did you come into it?'

'I was on the floor when it happened, and someone had to stop it. Then Mrs. Fleming looked so distraught that I offered to bring her back.'

'What were you doing at the *Lulu?*'

Mannering chuckled. 'Being a partner to Chloe! Apparently someone thinks I'm notorious enough to want to know, and Chloe's a friend of Chittering on the *Record*.'

'Oh, so he was there, was he?' Bristow sniffed expressively. 'Do you expect me to take all this at its face value?'

'Far be it from me to expect anything,' Mannering murmured blandly. 'Are you going to hold Fleming?'

'It's too early to say.'

'What about Mrs. Fleming?'

'Mortimer's sending a nurse in for her. She'll be all right. I wish I knew why you were interested in the Flemings, John. It couldn't be because this man Smith was burgled the other night, could it?'

Mannering looked blank.

'Was he? Who by?'

Bristow laughed, shortly.

There was nothing further for Mannering to stay for. He left the hotel without forming any conclusions, storing the facts both straightforward and curious. At the first telephone kiosk he called the *Lulu* Club. Lulu herself answered. She thought Mr. Chittering had said something about going to the office. He'd left soon after Mr. Mannering. Mr. Smith was still there. Mannering called the *Record*, and was told that Chittering had been in, but just gone out.

'When you find him, tell him to get in touch with the Milne Hotel, Knightsbridge as soon as possible.'

Mannering went outside. There were few

people about, but a straggle of late buses was rumbling along Kensington High Street. He got into the car, and drove through the dimly lit streets, parking eventually at the corner of Buckley Street.

Three quarters of an hour later, Paul Smith and Celia arrived in a taxi.

CHAPTER FOURTEEN

FRIENDLY VISIT

Mannering waited until the taxi had gone, then walked to Number 13. A light in the hall, visible through a small fanlight, went out. He lifted the knocker and let it fall with a hollow reverberation. Smith opened the door, the girl hovering in the dimly lit background.

'Good evening,' Mannering said, and stepped inside.

Smith barred his path.

'It's rather late for casual visitors,' he said shortly. 'Who are you?'

'We met at *Lulu's* tonight.'

Smith stood in shadow, allowing the light to fall on to Mannering's face. He stood utterly still, as if willing Mannering to withdraw.

Mannering said pleasantly, 'Delightful though circumlocutory preambles may be, I cannot help thinking that the time, the place, are a little ill-chosen when the police are at one's heels.'

Smith said dryly, 'Your heels or mine?' But he stood aside, nevertheless, and allowed

Mannering to close the door.

'Suppose we talk upstairs,' he said. 'My name is Mannering.'

'This is the second time tonight you've interfered with my private affairs.'

Mannering moved towards the stairs, the girl going before him. Smith followed. When they reached the first landing, Smith turned down a switch; for a moment they stood in utter darkness. Mannering's muscles tensed; he was prepared for anything. Another switch went down and a light shone out above them.

Smith laughed softly, with insolent understanding.

The girl reached the top landing, and turned right, towards the second flat. Mannering turned to follow her.

'Not that door,' Smith said.

'You're both in this,' said Mannering.

'We'll discuss it between us, first.'

'Oh, no,' said Mannering. 'It must be a threesome.'

Smith was now on a level with him.

'I *could* throw you out,' he said speculatively.

'Into the arms of the police, waiting for an excuse to interrogate you, yes,' said Mannering.

Smith said: 'You'd better come with us,

Celia, but leave when I tell you to.'

Automatically the girl turned, and came back, leading the way into the opposite flat. The electric fire was glowing, and the room struck warm. Smith closed the door and stood with his back against it and his hands in his pockets; too much the picture of nonchalance for it to be entirely real.

'Well, what's it all about?'

Mannering said deliberately: 'You had a difference of opinion with Miss Fleming's father this evening. I took him back to his hotel. In the room was a dead girl. She'd been strangled.'

Smith's smile faded and his lips set in a straight line. The girl moved forward with a shocked exclamation.

'Murdered,' Mannering said.

'Who—who was it?'

Smith said sharply: 'There'd be more point in asking what this has to do with us.'

Mannering said: 'Fleming quarrelled with you in front of a couple of hundred people. The police will want to know what that quarrel was about, bearing in mind that it might be linked with the murder.'

'Why?'

Mannering shrugged his shoulders.

'It does not need very much imagination to

foresee that Superintendent Bristow will be interested to learn that Fleming quarrelled with a man whose flat was mysteriously burgled recently.'

'Why did you trouble to come and warn me?'

'I thought you'd like to know.'

'What do you expect to get, in return?'

Mannering said: 'Personally, nothing. My interest is in Fleming. I don't believe he killed that girl, but I think he might find himself accused of it.'

'I couldn't care less.'

'Does that stand for Celia?' asked Mannering lightly.

'I hate him!' Celia's voice was low-pitched. 'I don't care what happens to him.'

'Is this all you've got to tell me?' Smith demanded.

'There is a little more. Fleming knew the girl.'

'Is that so.'

'So did you, if Fleming told the truth, and I think he did. The police are aware of this.'

Smith said gently: 'Now you're making it interesting.' He crossed to a cocktail cabinet. 'What will you have?'

'Whisky, please.'

'Celia?'

'Nothing,' she said, 'I think I've had enough tonight. Who was the dead girl?'

'The name is Muriel Lee,' Mannering said.

'No!' cried Celia.

Smith's hand was quite steady as he poured the drinks, and his voice was even as he added: 'Soda?'

'Please.'

'It couldn't be Muriel!' breathed Celia. 'Why, I saw her tonight, she was here—' she caught her breath.

'To the death of the murderer,' said Smith, raising his glass, 'Celia, darling, I think you'd better go and lie down. It's been a difficult evening for you.'

'I—I'd like to hear what happened.'

'I'll tell you, later.'

'Very well.' Without glancing to left or right, she walked automatically to the door. Smith opened it for her. He waited until the door opposite opened and closed, before returning to his chair.

'Now tell me why you came,' he said.

'I've told you. A friendly warning.'

'Why be friendly towards a stranger?'

'You never know when strangers might come in useful,' said Mannering. 'I wanted to get to know you better, anyhow. That was an impressive entry you made at *Lulu's* and I liked the way you behaved after Fleming took a smack at you.'

'I still haven't been told the truth,' said Smith.

'Possibly,' said Mannering, 'but you know as much as I'm going to tell you tonight. It's quite a lot. As Muriel was here earlier this evening, the police will have a double reason for wanting to see you. Also, they'll probably discover that you weren't at *Lulu*'s until late. They probably won't state in so many words that you had time to kill Muriel, but the suggestion will be there.'

'They'd be crazy if they thought that.'

'I've had a lot to do with the police,' Mannering said. 'Their craziness quite often pays off.' He finished his drink and went to the door. 'Mind if I go? I'd rather not be here when Bristow arrives. Of course, you could tell him that I've been, but that's up to you.'

He went to the door.

Smith said: 'I'd like to know what's in your mind.'

Mannering opened the door, slowly. 'I'm to be found at Quinn's by day—Hart Row, Bond Street—and River Walk, Chelsea, by night. If you want to know how to cope with Bill Bristow, let me know. I might even work for you, for a stiff retainer.'

He beamed, waved, and went out.

He heard the opposite door click; and knew that Celia had been listening.

No one was in the street when he reached it, and he drove straight to River Walk. There were no telephone messages. He left a note for Hetty, to say that he didn't want to be disturbed in the morning, and went to bed. He was curious but not dissatisfied. He owed Chittering a big debt; he had puzzled Smith, and would probably get a visit from him. He was likely to become a confidant of the Flemings, unless they were charged with murder, and he doubted whether Bristow would feel justified in taking that step yet.

Then he remembered he had forgotten his nightly call to Lorna.

★   ★   ★

Next morning, all the newspapers had the story of the murder, but the most detailed was in the *Record*. The article was signed: *Record Star Reporter*; Chittering had obviously been first on the spot. He had mentioned Mannering, like two of the other newspapers, but there was no mention of Smith or the incident at the club.

Mannering glanced through them all as he

drank his tea, and was thoughtful while he shaved. An unusually silent Hetty brought in his breakfast. There was no doubt she disapproved of these late nights while the mistress was away. At half-past ten Mannering telephoned Bristow.

'Now what is it?' Bristow was abrupt.

'How's Fleming?'

'You can read, can't you?' asked Bristow.

'But my papers don't say what happened after he'd been questioned.'

'He's at the Milne Court Hotel.'

'Good. But why so sharp with me, Bill?'

'One of these days I'll get sharper,' growled Bristow. 'I'm going to see you later in the day, anyhow. If you've any sense at all, you'll keep out of this affair.'

'I heard you,' Mannering said gently.

He did not believe that Smith had talked, but it was possible that Bristow had sent a man to watch Buckley Street, and that the man had taken the number of Mannering's car. He telephoned Major Fleming, but was told that he was not taking calls. He rang up Sylvester, was assured that there was nothing of importance in the post. It was eleven-fifteen when he entered the Milne Court Hotel.

None of the day staff recognised him, but

as he passed the open office door, the manager leapt to his feet.

'Mr. Mannering!'

Mannering waited, smiling.

'Mr. Mannering, have you come to see Major Fleming?'

'I'd like to.'

'He won't take telephone calls, he won't answer when we knock at his door. He's moving about, but—it's worrying, Mr. Mannering, very worrying.'

'Have you told the police?'

'I'm not sure that I'd be justified, although from our point of view the whole affair couldn't be more unfortunate.'

'Yes,' agreed Mannering. 'It couldn't be more unfortunate from the dead woman's point of view either. Where is Mrs. Fleming?'

'In her room, with a nurse—quite prostrate. *Quite* prostrate.'

'Thanks.' Mannering moved towards the lift, leaving the manager staring distractedly after him.

The second floor was deserted. He went to Fleming's room, and listened; there was no sound. A maid came along, looking at him curiously, and paused, as if she were about to speak. Mannering put a hand to his lips. The maid went past, and Mannering tapped sharply.

There was no response.

Mannering said: 'Fleming, this is Mannering. I want to see you.'

Immediately there was a move inside the room, and the key turned in the lock. Mannering expected to see a haggard man and saw instead that Fleming was spruce, distinguished, freshly shaven. There were scratches on his cheeks, and his right eye was slightly bloodshot, but these were the only signs of his daughter's attack.

He closed and locked the door.

'Why the precautions?' asked Mannering.

'I'm tired of being asked to find another hotel,' said Fleming brusquely. 'I shall do violence to that man if he comes again! I've enough on my mind. My wife's in a state of prostration. This murder is hanging over me, and—' he broke off, shrugging his shoulders. 'Mannering I'm extremely glad to see you. I doubt if the police will be persuaded that Smith knows anything about this murder. I'm quite sure that he will have an alibi. I'm equally sure that he committed it. If that could be proved, his hold over my daughter might be broken. Will you take the case?'

'Which comes first—proving Smith a murderer or saving Celia?'

'Celia.'

'I'll take the job,' said Mannering.

CHAPTER FIFTEEN

CELIA TAKES A TRIP

Fleming lit a cigarette, and smoked for some minutes without speaking. At last he said:

'That's a great relief. I believe you can do a lot that the police can't.'

'I didn't make any conditions, but there is one,' said Mannering. 'That you tell me all the truth.'

'Naturally.'

'Without any reservations. For instance, why are you so nervous of the police?'

'Wouldn't you be, in a spot like this?'

'That isn't your only reason. If it were, you'd be anxious but not really worried. If you didn't kill Muriel, you've nothing to fear in the long run, and you know it. Your nerves spring from one of two things—a guilty conscience or a skeleton in the cupboard.'

Fleming said stiffly: 'I'm not anxious that the police should probe too deeply into my domestic affairs.'

'Why not?'

'I suppose I'll have to tell you, Mannering, but I'm taking a chance. There is something that no one else knows, except one man. My wife—' Fleming hesitated, and when he went on, the words came reluctantly. 'My wife has a criminal record.'

That statement was so unexpected that Mannering simply said: 'Oh.'

'I thought it would surprise you.' Fleming's lips twisted wryly. 'I hope I needn't go into details. I didn't know it myself, at the time of our marriage. I didn't know until I saw an example of it, myself. I'm terrified, and I don't use the word lightly, in case the police take her fingerprints. Do you happen to know if Dominion criminal prints are held at Scotland Yard?'

'Not unless the criminal's been active over here, or the inquiries for him have been made here.'

'If you're sure, that's another relief,' said Fleming. 'Mannering, I know that my wife didn't kill Muriel, although you may not be so sure. I'd been with her, all the evening. We weren't separated for more than five minutes, at the *Lulu* Club. But she served a sentence of imprisonment for manslaughter in South Africa. When she has had too much to drink she loses her self-control completely. She isn't sane. I've had specialists, psychiatrists—they can do nothing. The only thing that helps is to stop her from drinking.' The words came out slowly and painfully. 'I hope you can see why I'm nervous.'

'And who is the other man who knows this? Smith?'

'Yes,' said Fleming.

'How has he used the knowledge?'

'Blackmail. It started with money, when we were in the same regiment. That is why I blame myself for Celia. I let them meet, and when Celia showed that she was being dominated by the man, I should have let him do his damnedest to me. Instead, I tried to reason with him. He stopped demanding money, and started to threaten that he would tell the truth about my wife unless I let him have his way with Celia. I thought he meant marriage.' Fleming laughed, harshly.

'Has your wife thrown any of these violent fits lately?'

'No. She's perfectly all right normally, but if she gets at the bottle—Mannering, I've known Celia deliberately set out to make her drunk. Smith's told Celia what to do, and she's obeyed him. She's no longer got a will of her own. God, how I hate that man!'

'Where do you think hate will get you?'

'Oh, you can talk. For years I've been repressing my feelings, keeping up a front, hoping that something would happen, that he'd tire of her—and all the time I'm getting nearer to boiling point. Lately, Smith has been sending messages through Muriel Lee.'

'What about?'

'Just reminding me to keep away from Celia. It's a sordid business, Mannering, but now you have the truth. I thought I'd hidden my fear pretty well. Do you think Bristow realised it?'

'Probably, but he almost certainly thinks that it's because you know more about the murder than you've said. What did Bristow say to you?'

'Not a great deal. He wanted to know my movements last night, and I told him everything, including the quarrel. He wanted to know how well I knew Muriel, and I said that she was a friend of my daughter. That's all. He asked me if I were planning to return to Guildford. I told him that until my wife was better, I would stay here.'

'Did he question you closely about your movements before you left the hotel, and when you returned?'

'Yes.'

'Why did you return—a little after ten o'clock?'

'My wife left her powder compact behind.'

'Did you both come back to find it?'

Fleming closed his eyes, and went into one of those long silences; and again Mannering waited patiently.

Then: 'I told Bristow that we both came back and both went into the room. That wasn't so. We both came up in the lift. I waited while my wife came along here for the compact. I didn't join her, because she was upset. She'd been reading over some of Celia's old letters, written before Smith took an interest in her. It upset her, and I know from experience that she recovers more quickly if she's on her own. She was here for about fifteen minutes I suppose. Bristow wanted to know why we took so long, and I made excuses. I—'

Mannering said abruptly: 'I think I'll change my mind, and leave you to work this one out for yourself.'

'Mannering!'

'Well, why not? If you're going to lie to me, what can I do to help?'

'But this is true. I'm telling you that Margaret could have—killed the girl.'

'Earlier, you said, you hadn't been separated except for five minutes at the *Lulu*.'

Fleming raised his hands and dropped them, in an almost pleading gesture.

'Yes, I know. It's so difficult to realise that I'm talking to someone I can trust and not to the police. But I've given you the whole story now, Mannering, this is true.'

Fleming's grey eyes were clouded and anxious. It robbed him of something of his good looks but didn't hide the likeness between him and his daughter. He had something of her intensity, too.

'Forget it,' Mannering said.

'You'll help?'

'I'll do what I can. And you've got to make sure that you tell the police exactly the same story today as you told them last night. There's one other danger, too—that when your wife recovers, she'll give a different explanation of the return visit.'

'I don't think she will,' said Fleming. 'I think it's the true one. I know it *is* possible that she came back here and saw Muriel, but she wasn't drunk or anything like it, she was just upset by reading those old letters. The police have a nurse with her, of course, as soon as she's fit enough to make a statement, they'll get it, but we've nothing to worry about with that. I'm convinced that Smith killed Muriel.'

'Just to turn the screw on you?'

Fleming laughed; and it was an ugly sound.

'Oh, not just that. I told you I hated him. He hates me, just as much. He knows that I'll never stop trying to win Celia back. He also knows I'll try to prove that he's a rogue and a thief. I've made him look a fool in public several times, I'm doing all I can to make him lose his temper, if he once does that, he'll start to weaken. After the last occasion, he said he'd put me where I couldn't do him any more harm. This is what he meant.'

'It could be,' Mannering said. 'I wouldn't rate the chance very high. If he killed Muriel, it was because he wanted to get rid of her, and he framed you as an incidental. He took a big risk, if he actually did it. Is there anyone else who's playing this hate game with you?'

'No.'

'Do you know anyone else who's working with him?'

'Only a woman, a kind of housekeeper. Mrs. Morant—she's quite harmless, as far as I know.

'What was the relationship between Smith and Muriel?'

'I don't really know. Probably she was his secretary.'

'He has a legitimate job, then?'

'Oh yes, some kind of a mail order business. Personally, I think it's a blind.'

'Do you know for a fact he's a thief?'

'Indeed I do. He rifled the Mess funds. I made good the losses. That's how it started—I found out what he'd done and was going to report, and he told me that he knew about Margaret, my wife. It's seven years ago, now,' Fleming said. 'Seven years. If it weren't for Celia, I think I'd have killed myself long before this.'

'Well, if you commit suicide now, you'll be confessing to the murder of Muriel Lee,' said Mannering, 'so think again. Will you let me know when next Bristow come to see you, and make a careful note of the questions he asks?'

'Yes, of course.'

'Now, if I were you, I'd go and have a breath of fresh air,' said Mannering.

★ ★ ★

He left Fleming at the entrance to Hyde Park, and drove to Quinn's. He was there for only half an hour, warned Sylvester that he might not be in much during the next few days, then drove to Larraby's hotel. Larraby was in a small, pleasant room, looking rested and refreshed.

'Feeling better?' Mannering asked.

'A new man,' said Larraby. 'What can I

do?'

'Find someone reliable to watch Smith and Celia Fleming,' said Mannering, 'and also try to trace a Muriel Lee, who worked for Smith, anything else you can about her.'

'And after that?'

'Sleep some more,' said Mannering, and left Larraby smiling with satisfaction.

He drove to the *Record* office, and found Chittering in the middle of a vast room, surrounded by myriads of typewriters and telephones, all in violent operation. He alone was motionless, leaning back with his eyes closed and a half-smoked cigarette jutting from his underlip.

Mannering said: 'You're as bad as Larraby.'

'Never,' said Chittering, opening one eye. 'He has a great regard for you. Good morning, John. Thanks for the tip last night.'

'Pleasure. How is Chloe?'

'She telephoned half an hour ago. Apparently she and Jane adored their evening out. They could mean it.'

'Didn't you say they live together in a cottage in the country?'

Chittering opened the other eye.

'Yes. Why?'

'What are they really like?'

'Oh, quite human,' said Chittering. 'In fact, nice. They're District Nurses, you know, near Winchester. Once home of King Alfred.'

'Discreet, loyal and trustworthy?'

Chittering leaned forward. 'What is all this?'

'If I wanted to hide, or someone wanted to hide, would they play?'

'I think Chloe would do practically anything you asked, short of murder,' said Chittering. 'Who's running from the law?'

'No one, yet. Will you warn them that such an event might happen?'

'Yes, indeed. It will make their day. Do you mean to say that's all you want?'

Mannering laughed.

'Not quite, Chitty. I'm anxious to learn what I can about Muriel Lee, who died last night—you know she worked for Smith, I presume? And I'd like to know what Bristow has been doing at Buckley Street.'

That's better,' said Chittering. 'He's been asking lots of questions, but he hasn't got anywhere. He is probably coming after you with an axe, too. He had a man watching Buckley Street, and knows you went to see Smith. He can't understand why you wanted to warn the chap of what had happened. I think you made a mistake, John. Until then, Bristow was radiating friendliness and goodwill towards you, but this has got under his skin.'

'Don't we live by mistakes?' asked Mannering lightly.

'And frequently die by them,' Chittering said. 'I'll send a note about Muriel Lee when I've got all the dope.'

'Between us,' said Mannering, 'we'll probably hit the front page headlines one of these days.'

Chittering was still seeking for a Parthian shot of sufficient deadliness when Mannering reached the doors. He drove straight to Chelsea. The Yard man was watching from the house opposite, but no one had followed him. He realized that Bristow was trying to cramp him. It was a pity Bristow had discovered that he had warned Smith, but the dividend from the warning would probably be big, if there was any at all.

He let himself into the flat.

The dividend came hurrying across the hall towards him—Celia Fleming, smothered in mink.

CHAPTER SIXTEEN

SOFT SPOT

She didn't say anything as Mannering closed the door, just stopped in front of him, one hand outstretched and touching his. The kitchen door opened, and Hetty began to speak.

'Oh, Mr. Mannering, there's a lady who—' She broke off, staring at Celia in disapproval.

'All right, Hetty, thanks.'

As Hetty withdrew, Mannering took Celia's arm, and led her into the study. Beneath the make-up, there were signs of strain, but none, that he could recognise, of drugs.

He moved away from her.

'What is it, Miss Fleming?'

She said slowly: 'How is my mother?'

'Badly shaken, but not seriously ill.'

'Are you sure?'

'I was told so, this morning.'

She turned from him, and he thought it was because tears had sprung to her eyes. She stared, unseeing, at the window.

'Can I give her a message?'

'Tell her, please, that I inquired.'

'I will.'

She hadn't come for this alone, but now that she was here, she couldn't bring herself to divulge the paramount reason.

'Why did she do it?' she asked abruptly.

'Do what?'

'Kill Muriel.'

'What makes you think she did?'

'Of course she did!'

'I still don't know what makes you think so?'

'She's—violent—sometimes.'

'She wasn't violent and she wasn't drunk last night. You ought to know that. Did Paul suggest that she'd killed Muriel?'

Celia bit her lips.

'So he did. Are you ever going to wake up to the fact that what Paul says might not always be true?'

'Oh, it's true enough!'

'Did you tell the police this?'

'Of course I didn't!' Her sudden anger drove away some of her fear, making her more natural. 'Of course I didn't!'

'Did Paul?'

'I didn't come here to discuss Paul.'

'Why did you come?'

'I wanted to find out how she was. I wanted—' she broke off again. 'That's all. Thank you.'

'It isn't quite enough,' said Mannering, and went across and took her hands. 'Look at me, Celia.' She avoided his eyes. 'Look at me,' he repeated gently, and she obeyed, but the fear was back; she was frightened of him, and perhaps also of something else. 'Celia, why did you come to see me? What do you want from me?'

'Nothing!'

'That's not true.' His pressure on her hands increased. 'Tell me. I won't pass it on.'

'There's nothing,' she said, and wrenched herself free. 'I must go. I shouldn't have come. Just give that message to my mother.' She reached the door and opened it, and as she walked across the hall, the front door bell rang. Mannering didn't think she heard it. She fumbled with the latch and had the door open before Mannering could help her. She pulled it wide and stepped blindly out—and a man stretched out a hand and pushed her back.

It was Paul Smith.

He didn't look at Mannering, Smith closed the door with one hand, then suddenly moved the other, and slapped her across the face. It wasn't a hard blow, but she cringed back, as if in terror.

Smith slid his hands into his pockets.

'What did she come to see you about Mannering?'

Mannering said: 'I don't know. She changed her mind about talking.' He went to Smith's side and, without haste, closed his fingers round the man's right forearm. Smith grinned, nastily, and tensed his muscles; then Mannering gripped and twisted, and Smith gasped with sudden pain. He shot back against the wall as Mannering released him.

Celia, who had flown like a wildcat at her father when he had laid a hand on this man, didn't move.

Smith straightened up and shrugged his coat into position.

'Somehow I don't think we're going to be good friends,' he said. 'You don't seem to have done any harm, Celia, we'll go now.'

'Not just yet,' said Mannering.

'I'll go when I want to,' Smith said. His voice sharpened with a note of command. 'Celia!'

She moved towards the door, without thought or volition. The man was watching her. Mannering frowned as he looked from one to the other. Celia's hand moved slowly, reluctantly, but she opened the door and stepped onto the landing. Smith started to follow.

'Not you,' Mannering said.

Smith's lip lifted in a sneer.

Mannering said: 'Maybe I can use hypnotism, too.'

Smith started, and turned round. The girl went on. Mannering closed the door behind her, and, ignoring Smith, went to the study. By the time he was sitting at the desk, Smith was at the door. The two men stood looking at each other, in a strange conflict of wills.

Then Smith laughed.

'You get some fool notions,' he said. 'I suppose it's no use reasoning with you. Celia's just a dope. But she's wonderful to look at, and that isn't the only way she's good. She'll do what I tell her, I don't have to use any funny stuff with her. Forget it.'

'Not yet,' said Mannering. 'but we'll talk about something else.'

'What?'

'Apart from wanting to see Celia, why did you come here?'

'Now you're thought reading. Why are you so interested in me, Mannering?'

'Strong personalities always fascinate me.'

'Only that?'

'Should there be anything else?'

'I don't know,' said Smith. 'Possibly you think we might be able to do some business together.'

'What kind of business?'

Smith stared with that curious intensity, as if he were wishing to read Mannering's thoughts. He was making a conscious mental effort, and there was stillness in the room. Mannering felt the sense of strain and knew, beyond all doubt, where Smith drew his power to influence others as he had influenced Celia.

Smith looked away, and shrugged.

'I still think you might be interested in a business arrangement, but I'd like to find out why you think so. Come and see me again.'

'I will,' said Mannering.

Smith turned and went out. The front door closed softly, and there was no other sound. Mannering drew a hand across his forehead, and it came away damp. He hadn't enjoyed those last few minutes, and had a feeling that he might have given something away that he wanted to keep to himself. He rejected the thought, but it persisted.

Hetty came in, nervously.

'Has the gentleman gone, sir?'

'Yes.'

'I hope *he* doesn't come very often,' Hetty said, with the frankness of guileless, undisciplined youth. 'Will you be in to lunch?'

'Yes, Hetty—say half past one.'

'It'll be on time,' said Hetty.

She hadn't liked Smith, even on that brief acquaintance; had instinctively felt that there was corruption in him. Yet when Smith could have used vicious methods, with him and Larraby, he'd rejected them. Was that contradictory evidence or simply a matter of tactics?

Mannering ate a hearty lunch, and then shaking off lethargy, walked briskly to Victoria. It took him half an hour. He went on by taxi to the Post Office near Trafalgar Square, and turned to the *poste restante* counter.

'Mr. J. Brown?' asked the clerk, and went through a small bundle of letters. 'Oh, yes, there is one.' She slipped the letter beneath the grille, and Mannering opened it before he went away. It was from Smith, who signed himself 'C', and the address was 60, Palling Street, S.E.1. (the Palling Garage). It read:

Come and see me again, any evening between six thirty and seven o'clock. I think we could do business together.

Mannering tore the letter up and dropped the pieces into a waste paper basket. He went out and walked purposefully towards Scotland Yard. It was then half past three. The policemen on duty at the Criminal Investigation Department building did not stop him and he went straight up to Bristow's office.

He tapped.

'Come in,' called Bristow.

He was sitting at his desk, glancing through some papers, and the telephone bell rang as Mannering opened the door. Bristow picked up the receiver and then saw Mannering. He glared.

'Oh, it's you, is it. I want you.' There was hostility in his eyes as Mannering entered, and he continued to look at Mannering as he spoke into the telephone. 'Ask him to ring up later, I don't want disturbing for the next half hour.'

He put the receiver down with a bang.

CHAPTER SEVENTEEN

BRISTOW'S HIGH HORSE

No one else was in the office, and Mannering drew up a chair. The window was open, and Bristow shut it with cold precision. Standing with his back towards it, his face in shadow, his expression of hostility was hardly concealed.

'You damned fool,' he said.

'If you say so.'

'Until you've been inside, I don't suppose you'll ever learn.'

'I repeat, if you say so.'

'Haven't you the sense not to keep getting in our way?'

'Perhaps I don't know where you're going.'

'You know where we're going all right. It was crazy to go and warn Smith that we were likely to visit him. If he's had anything to do with that murder, it gave him time to get ready for us.'

'But you always catch guilty men.'

'If we did,' Bristow said roughly, 'we'd have caught you long ago. But you'll find yourself in dock yet, never fear, and probably for something you didn't do.'

'Rough justice at the Yard! Why the high horse, Bill?'

'Isn't this enough? You warned Smith and the Fleming girl. You then went to Major Fleming, and did something to him—he's twice as difficult to handle. You had visits from Smith and the girl, too.'

'Where's the criminal offence?'

'You're obstructing us.'

'Oh, no. Trying to help you.'

Bristow said: 'Listen to me. I know you were at Smith's flat the other night. The description tallied with the description we've had before when you've been about. That means you committed an offence and could be sent down for three years, or more. You get too damned cocky. And you assaulted several of our men.'

'Someone did,' said Mannering.

'You did.'

'Let's draw a veil over that,' said Mannering. 'What do you think I'm doing with Smith?'

'I don't know yet. But I can tell you, you're going to burn your fingers before it's over. Smith is dynamite. And he's bad.'

'A point of agreement at last.'

'Why interfere in this job?'

'I thought I was invited to help find the Shadow.'

'Forget it.'

'It stirred up my curiosity.'

Bristow said in a milder voice: 'What makes you think there's any connection between Smith and the Shadow?'

'I'm just wondering.'

'You know something that's material evidence. Don't withhold it.'

'Not for a split second, when I think you could use it,' said Mannering. 'Bill, I came to tell you several things, one of them to beware Smith, and to find out what he was doing on the nights that the Shadow was busy. If he's the Shadow, I'd like to see him inside.'

'Don't you know if he is or not?'

'No. Do you?'

Bristow said: 'I know that he was out on each of the Shadow's jobs.'

'We progress,' said Mannering.

'The Fleming girl gives him an alibi for three of the nights.'

'Poor Celia.'

'And she frequently goes to Paris.'

'It's fairly obvious that she buys her clothes there.'

'She could take the stolen stuff over, and sell it—we haven't traced any unloading of what the Shadow stole, in England. I don't say that happened, but it could have done. Muriel Lee was also in the habit of slipping over to the Continent—she had friends in Brussels. Did you know all this?'

'You're telling me, Bill.'

'I'm as crazy as you are,' Bristow said, and quite suddenly, he laughed. It was a good laugh to hear. Laughter, at the unexpected moment, was one of Bristow's saving graces.

'John, listen to me.' He offered cigarettes from a yellow packet. 'I know you wouldn't touch anything this man Smith does with a barge-pole. I think you're doing what you think is best, but you're asking for trouble. At the beginning of this affair, I had Anderson-Kerr sympathetic about asking your help. Now he's dead against it. You'll run yourself up against the Yard every time you move. Don't be a bigger fool than you can help.'

'There may not be much difference,' Mannering said, smiling. 'Have you discovered Smith's other name and business yet?'

Bristow stopped in the act of lighting a cigarette.

'What? I—oh, that. Yes.' He concentrated with unnecessary energy on lighting a cigarette. 'Of course we have.'

'I just wanted to make sure,' said Mannering. 'As you know, I needn't tell you. 'Bye, Bill.'

Bristow jumped towards him.

'John—'

'Appointment,' beamed Mannering. 'Very remiss of me. I want to sell a diamond to a millionaire.'

Bristow didn't follow him out of the office; and Bristow hadn't yet got round to the fact that Smith was Caton of the Palling Street Garage.

★ ★ ★

At the flat, there was a note from Chittering. Did Mannering know that Celia Fleming often went to Paris, that Muriel Lee had as often gone to Brussels, and that the Yard thought that there was a connection between Smith and the Shadow. In a post-script the reporter said that Chloe and Jane would 'play'.

★ ★ ★

There was a change in the tactics of the police, and one for the worse. When he left Chelsea, Mannering was tailed. It did not greatly worry him, but it meant that from the moment he had disappeared, there would be an alert throughout the police stations of London.

He missed the Buick.

He slipped his tailer near Piccadilly, and then went to a little shop in the Edgware Road, where Old Sol, a man who specialised in theatrical make-up and wig-making, greeted him warmly. Three quarters of an hour later he left the shop in a different suit and a professional make-up which was infinitely better than that he had used the first night. He went to an all night garage, and, using the shopkeeper's name for a reference, hired a self-driven car, a roomy and powerful Austin. He drove to Southwark, and parked the car a hundred yards from Palling's Garage. He walked the rest of the way, arriving at twenty minutes to seven.

The big man was outside, working on the only taxi there. He was still in his shirt-sleeves. Mannering knocked at the side door. It was opened almost immediately by a small, thin-faced man, who led the way upstairs. Mannering was left on the landing for two minutes, until the other returned. 'He'll see you.'

Mannering used the harsh voice with which Smith would be familiar. The fact that he didn't look the same man wasn't important, Smith had known that he was disguised, before.

The room Mannering was taken to was a bed-sitter, well furnished, with several touches of luxury. A television stood in one corner, and there was a radiogram in another. There were two deep armchairs in front of an electric fire, and Smith was sitting in one of them. Reclining, with his legs stretched out in front of him, he looked abnormally tall. His lips were turned down in the familiar sneering smile.

'So you can read,' he said.

'I can read.' Mannering pushed the door to in the face of the little man.

'And don't you love playing at being clever,' said Smith. 'That make-up wouldn't deceive a flat foot.'

'You'd do better if you played at it too, a little more assiduously. Supposing the police find out you're here?'

'They won't. Come and sit down. Have a drink?'

'No.'

'It's not poisoned.'

'If you say so.'

'You're too suspicious,' Smith said. 'I told you I wouldn't start any reprisals. Any man who can do the job you did the other night, sounds good to me. Where did you learn how to crack a crib?'

'I've been at it all my life.'

'And got away with it.'

'I'm here, aren't I? What are we wasting time for? What do you want?'

'I talked about a business partnership.'

'*That's* more like it,' Mannering said. 'Anything I do, I do fifty-fifty.'

'It suits me. Ever heard of the Shadow?'

Mannering's expression didn't change.

'That reminds me of something,' he said.

Smith chuckled.

'Well, the Shadow gets away with a lot of good stuff, but he isn't, I should judge, any better than you are at it, professionally. He just knows where to go.'

'I can do any job. The difficulty is to sell the stuff without the necessary contacts,' Mannering admitted. 'I don't trust receivers. They're all right on commercial stuff, but the police are always at them on jewellery, that's why I kept off it.'

'I can sell it,' Smith said quietly.

'How do I know you'll give me an even split?'

'You just have to trust me—but you'll be satisfied. You'll know the value of the stuff you've taken, won't you? And you'll know what you ought to get for it. I can sell in the right markets. Want to hear any more?'

'It won't hurt me to listen.'

Smith chuckled again. 'You're a hard case,' he said. 'It'll do you a lot of good to listen, Brown, provided you listen carefully. You could do the jobs in exactly the same way as the Shadow does them and he'll be blamed for it. They won't be looking for you, they'll be looking for him.'

'Supposing he's out on a job the same night?'

'He won't be,' Smith said. 'I've some influence there.'

'Cut it out,' Mannering said. 'You *are* the Shadow. What do you think I've been having you watched for? Electric appliances?' He sneered. 'Every night in the past two months that the Shadow's done a job, you've been out. Own up—I only deal with principals.'

Smith said softly: 'I am a principal. I can't stop you from guessing. I'm putting a straightforward proposal to you—do some jobs with me, I'll sell the stuff, and we'll split fifty-fifty.'

'And what if I'm caught?'

'That's your risk.'

'I'd get a lagging for being the Shadow,

which I'm not.'

Smith said: 'You ought to have had that drink.' He stood up uncoiling himself slowly, and his glittering eyes grew sharper. Mannering felt uneasy: could Smith guess that Brown was Mannering? There was nothing on Smith's face to suggest that he had realised it. He was intent again on subjugating another's will.

Mannering licked his lips, and looked away.

'Don't glare at me like that!' He sounded nervous.

'Look at me,' said Smith, gently.

'Why should I?' The compelling gaze that met his own was uncanny. Mannering felt much as he had done at Chelsea and again he wondered whether indeed it was Smith who was being fooled, or himself.

'You don't *have* to work with me,' Smith said. 'But it's easy money. You won't have to worry about selling, I'll take all the risks once the stuff is on our hands. I'll give you different addresses to take it to, every time. One night a week, and you can live like a Prince for the rest of the time. You'd be a fool to turn it down. But before we call it a deal, Mister Brown, I want to know who you are.'

Mannering muttered: 'I don't trust anybody as much as that.'

'You could be a split.'

'Me, a busy? Don't be crazy.'

'You could be,' Smith said. 'I don't think you are, but there's a risk. I'm taking that, you've got to take the other. Otherwise—' he didn't finish, but laughed; and the laugh carried a menace which seemed to strike back at Mannering from the walls. 'I'll fix you,' he said. 'Who are you?'

CHAPTER EIGHTEEN

THE DEAL

Mannering stood up, ignoring Smith's steady, almost fluorescent, glare. Without removing his gloves, he poured himself a drink, tossing down a generous tot of whisky.

'You needed that,' Smith said.

'I don't know that I want to work with you,' said Mannering, still feigning nervousness. 'I'll think about it. If you won't be satisfied without knowing my real name, maybe the risk is too big.'

'I won't be satisfied.'

'I'll think about it,' Mannering muttered.

Smith said: 'Don't take too long.'

Mannering went out, conscious of the other's gaze even when his back was turned. He had a feeling of imminent danger, as he had had when going upstairs at Buckley Street with this man behind him. But when Mannering glanced round Smith was still standing motionless, the curl of the thin lips and the glow in the glittering eyes suggesting that he was laughing at some satanic joke.

Mannering was glad when the door closed.

The little man was nowhere in sight. He let himself out, and walked slowly to the Austin. Before he had gone a hundred yards, he knew that he was being followed. There was a taxi standing outside the garage, and its engine started up. Mannering didn't quicken his pace. By the time he was at the Austin, the taxi was in sight. He did not look round or show that he knew he was being followed. He drove carefully back across Blackfriars Bridge, then through the West End until he was at the Edgware Road. He parked the car in a side street and walked along to Old Sol's.

The taxi was on the other side of the road, and the man following him was walking.

Sol's shop was shut. Mannering rang the bell, and had to wait for two minutes, before it was opened. His shadower pretended to be looking into the window of a restaurant.

Sol opened the door himself, a small man with a wizened face and a beaked nose.

'Back so soon, my friend?' He stood aside, invitingly.

In a room at the rear of the shop, which looked like a cross between a barber's shop and a theatre dressing-room, he stood waiting expectantly, expecting to be asked to remove the disguise. When Mannering didn't speak, the old man's face grew anxious.

'Is there trouble, bad trouble?'

'Not yet, Sol. I want a flat or a house, a small place, to which I can go straight away, and be readily accepted as a Mr. John Brown. And if inquiries are made, I want it to be said that I've lived in the place for a long time and am a salesman for a big company.'

The veiny old eyes were sombre.

'Will the police be inquiring?'

'No, Sol, just a bad man who thinks I may be fooling him.'

The smile came back.

'Then that is quite easy, my friend. I shall make a telephone call, and then give you the address.'

* * *

The address was of a small house in Paddington. Mannering arrived half an hour later, was received by a middle-aged woman as if she knew him well, and went inside. From a front room, he watched the street. The man who had followed him there, and a little later, knocked at the front door. The woman opened it. Mannering didn't hear what she said, but Smith's man went off, after ten minutes or so, and both he and the taxi driver left the street.

Mannering arranged to be able to call whenever he wanted, and left five pounds with the middle-aged woman.

* * *

It was too soon to return to the garage; in any case, Smith probably wouldn't be there. Mannering went to Chelsea, after another visit to Old Sol, who removed the make-up. Dressed in his own clothes and driving the Sunbeam Talbot, Mannering went to Chelsea. He waved across the street to the invisible man who was watching. Bristow would know by now, and there would be a careful scrutiny of all the jobs done that night; and Bristow would get nothing for this pains.

He whistled as he went upstairs, taking out his keys. But the door opened before he reached it, and Lorna stood there.

* * *

Mannering lifted her off her feet, kissed her, then carried her across the hall. He dropped into an armchair with Lorna in his lap, and kissed her again.

'I have a lot of lipstick on,' she said coldly.

'Who cares about a little lipstick at a time

like this?'

'Better now than at the *Lulu* Club,' Lorna said.

'Didn't you wear any then?'

'I'm not talking about the time when you went with your lawful wife. What woman have you been taking about?'

'Oh, Chloe!' Mannering laughed. 'You ought to see Chloe. You probably will, too, I'm going to dance with her at least once again before I die. Darling, you look wonderful. How's mother?'

'Better. She is very like me in that she doesn't trust you when you're on your own.'

'The firm belief of practically all women. The strange thing is that any men survive.'

'John,' said Lorna, 'be serious. I arrived an hour ago. Bristow came five minutes afterwards. If I can believe him, there is likely to be a warrant out for your arrest any time.'

'Don't believe him.'

'I want to know what you've been doing.'

'And you shall,' said Mannering warmly.

* * *

It was a relief to talk, and Lorna, as always, was a good listener. She poured him out a whisky and soda, when he'd finished.

'And all for this Celia,' she said.

'In point of fact you're wrong there. Lovely though she is, I see her only as an unexpected twist in an already tortuous journey. When it's over, we'll know the Shadow, we'll know the truth about Smith, and we may or may not have taken Major Fleming out of his particular kind of purgatory. Quite a lot at one sweep.'

'You already know the Shadow,' said Lorna.

'Ah,' said Mannering.

'Don't you?'

'I've a pretty good idea.'

'You're quite hopeless. I guessed what was happening, of course, that's why I couldn't keep away. I needn't go back, either.'

'Pity,' said Mannering.

'Thank you, darling.'

'Because I'm going away for a day or two.'

'We are.'

'Humph.'

'Where are we going?'

'First of all to Guildford, to have a look at Major Fleming's happy home. Then to Winchester, to see Chloe. We may go on to Paris, after that. Suit you?'

Lorna laughed. 'When you're mysterious with me, I know you're feeling cockahoop.'

'I'm not that far on yet,' Mannering assured her, 'but I see possibilities of feeling it. I—that would happen now.'

It was the telephone.

Lorna answered it, whipping up the receiver just before he reached it. After a while, she said:

'Yes, he's here.'

'Who?' asked Mannering urgently.

'Toby Plender.'

Mannering took the receiver from her. 'Hallo, Toby.'

'Have you seen Bristow?' asked Plender abruptly. 'He's on the warpath.'

'That was before I saw him, this afternoon.'

'Oh, you've seen him, have you?' Plender sounded relieved. 'He seemed to be pretty sure that you'd run yourself into trouble. I thought you might want me to defend you.'

'Not me. Toby—'

'Hm-hm?'

'You've read about the Muriel Lee case, haven't you? And the Flemings?'

'And that you were there.'

'Care to lend a hand?'

'If it's legal, yes.'

'Right. I want you to cross-examine Fleming, in the nicest possible way. I'll send you a note, telling you what he told me, and I'd like you to shake his story if you can. If you can't, I'll be inclined to believe it.'

'If I can't shake it, it's true,' said Plender. 'When is this to be?'

'I'll tell him you're lending a hand, and give you a letter of introduction,' Mannering said.

'All right. Delighted to hear Lorna's back. She seems to be the only one who can do anything with you.' Plender laughed and rang off.

Mannering smoothed down his hair and looked at Lorna with thoughtful eyes. She was looking her best, and although she so strongly disapproved, he thought that she was feeling something of his excitement.

He went forward, and kissed her. She was breathless when he let her go.

The telephone bell rang again.

'My turn,' said Mannering, and picked up the receiver. 'Hallo.'

It was Chittering.

'Oh, hallo,' repeated Mannering, with more enthusiasm. 'How's Chloe?'

'I don't wear her on a chain,' said Chittering mildly. 'She'll do what you want, why worry about it any more? I think I have an inkling of what you're up to, John. You're a crafty devil.'

'Thanks.'

'I thought this would interest you, too,' said Chittering. 'Smith has bought a ticket for the mid-day 'plane to Paris, tomorrow. It is in the name of Celia Fleming. I can't tell you whether someone else will go in her place, but personally I should think that he's sending her away.'

'It wouldn't surprise me if you were right,' said Mannering.

'I know. Anything I can do to help?'

'Yes,' said Mannering. 'You could telephone Smith, and put the fear of death into him. Get him away from his flat and make sure that he stays away for a couple of hours—oh, and telephone me when you know he's swallowed your bait.'

'I see,' said Chittering. 'And what are you going to do?'

'Have a chat with Celia.'

'It's a good job you're a grass widower.'

'That's all spoilt,' said Mannering, and rang off.

He turned and looked at Lorna more seriously, and she saw that there was calculating slant in his expression, could guess at the wildness of the thoughts that were passing through his mind. There was devilment there, a flash of the daring and recklessness which she'd first seen and first begun to love.

'Well,' she said.

'I think you could help on this job,' said Mannering. 'You could give her confidence. If she knew I trusted my wife with her, she'd feel much safer.'

'Who? Celia Fleming?'

'Of course.'

'What is your plan?'

'Next to nothing. I've been conning over the best way of making her boy friend really angry. The most obvious, and the most likely to succeed would be to abscond with Celia. Just a little gentle job of kidnapping. Of course, you don't *have* to come.'

CHAPTER NINETEEN

KIDNAPPING

Mannering pulled up outside 13 Buckley Street, and leaned across Lorna to open the door.

'We're here,' Mannering announced portentously.

'I don't see how you're going to do it,' Lorna said. 'But what I do see is that you're taking a crazy chance.'

'How?'

'Everyone knows you're here. The police car followed us, it's round the corner now. You said yourself that a man is watching the flat—I can see him.' She gazed coldly at the crown of an unmoving hat. 'Even if you managed to take Celia Fleming away, everyone would know who did it.'

'But this is to be a kidnapping with a difference,' Mannering murmured. 'We mustn't waste time. Chittering may not be able to hold our Mr. Smith very long, and it's already half an hour since he telephoned.'

'I'm not moving from here until I know what you're going to do.'

Mannering's hand closed over hers.

'You worry too much. I'm going to ask Celia to come away with us. I shan't use force, only persuasion.'

'She simply won't come!'

'Even you'll admit that there's no harm in trying.'

With an air of holding a great many things she wished to say in reserve, Lorna got out.

The man in the unmoving hat had drawn it out of sight, but another, probably from the police car which had followed them, stood at the corner. The night was quiet and still. Here and there the yellow square of a lighted window stood out. The crooning of a love song came very faintly from a distant radio.

Mannering rang the bell.

Lorna, like an over-tried but persistent guardian angel, stood by Mannering's side. Even in the gloom, something could be seen of the devil-may-care look on his face.

A light flicked on.

'Supposing Smith is back already,' suggested Lorna.

Mannering grunted.

A woman opened the door. He guessed her to be Mrs. Morant. Plump and fluffy-haired, there was a hint of nervousness in her voice.

'Good evening.'

'Good evening,' said Mannering. 'Is Miss Fleming in?'

'Well, she is, but she can't see anyone. She's resting.'

'She'll see me,' said Mannering, authoritatively.

'She won't see *any*one.' The woman's voice wavered.

Mannering smiled.

'She will, you know.'

Hardly aware that she was in retreat, the woman backed before him. Lorna slipped in after him, and closed the door. Mrs. Morant's lips parted. One call would have brought the police to her aid, but she stood inertly against the wall, in a state of nervous hesitation.

'Nobody told me you were coming.'

'It's a surprise visit,' said Mannering. 'I've been here before, but will you lead the way up?'

'I'm not really sure that I ought to let you come up,' said Mrs. Morant, satisfying her own sense of indecision by this remark. Propelled upward, at each landing she turned and looked at Mannering, but didn't speak. Arriving at a part of the flat he hadn't yet visited, Mannering saw that the door was ajar.

'If you'll just wait here, I'll see if she's presentable, she wouldn't like—'

Mannering's beaming smile cut across Mrs. Morant's vagaries as he pushed the door open. This flat appeared to be made on exactly the same layout as the one opposite. Even the furniture was a replica.

Mrs. Morant, twittering half finished sentences, hurried towards the door which, across the landing, would have led to the study. As she did so, Celia appeared.

She wore a scarlet housecoat, expensively plain, and without trimming. Against it, her face seemed almost transparently white. Only her hair, curling inwards, gave the necessary touch of substance.

'Oh, Celia *dar*ling, the gentleman wouldn't wait downstairs, I did ask him to.'

Mrs. Morant backed away, faintly wringing her hands.

'Hallo,' said Mannering, brightly. 'May I present my wife?'

Celia looked at Lorna long and steadily. She took no notice of Mrs. Morant. Like her father, she seemed to have a habit of long silences. She was calmer than she had been at Chelsea.

'What is it?' she asked.

'I've a message from your mother.'

Celia started. Tension came to her, and with it, alarm.

'What message, please?'

'She wants to see you.'

'Oh, *no!*' cried Mrs. Morant, 'you mustn't leave here, Celia darling, you know Paul doesn't like you to go out without telling him first. And you've that long journey in the morning!'

For all the notice Celia took, she need not have spoken.

'Where is my mother?' asked Celia.

'At the Milne Court Hotel, Knightsbridge.'

'You said this morning that she wasn't seriously ill.'

'She is, now. She wants to see you.'

'But you mustn't go out!' cried Mrs. Morant.

Celia took notice, this time; and the change in her was astonishing. She smiled; he hadn't seen her smile before. It gave life and freshness to her beauty, and it made her seem much younger. She moved quickly to Mrs. Morant, and took her hands.

'Ethel, he needn't know, need he? I could just slip out and be back within an hour— Paul said he wouldn't be home until after midnight. He needn't know, if you don't tell him.' She squeezed the older woman's hands, as if she were humouring a child. 'I'll be able to help you, one day, to make up for it. Be a pet, and go and take out a suit—any one will do.' She brushed Mrs. Morant's overpowdered cheeks with her lips, and then gave her a little push. Mrs. Morant hesitated, but eventually went to the door.

'Supposing he should find out,' she said waveringly.

'But he needn't, Ethel, unless you're silly, and I know you can keep a confidence.'

'Well—'

'You'd better make it the black suit,' Celia said.

Mrs. Morant disappeared, but left the door open. As Celia went across and closed it the long glowing housecoat lent added grace to her movements. There was eagerness in her manner when she hurried across to Mannering.

'Is she terribly ill, or—'

'I thought you'd like to see her and I knew that Paul was out.'

She didn't ask how he knew.

'I won't be five minutes,' she said, and turned and hurried into the bedroom. There were sounds of voices and movement, and once Celia laughed; the laugh certainly couldn't have come from Mrs. Morant.

Lorna said: 'What is going to happen when she realizes that she isn't going to see her mother?'

Mannering said: 'But she is.'

Lorna took a deep breath, 'And after that, what?'

'That's when we do the kidnapping,' Mannering said. 'Unless Celia has changed her ways, she'll come out dripping in mink. She'll go into the hotel dripping in mink. You will come out, wrapped in the same mink, and she will have your outfit on. Close observers will then see me and a woman they believe to be my wife, drive off. I shall shake off the police car, get into another, and drive to Chloe's cottage. You will drive the bus outside, and the police call sent out for it will quickly be rewarded. You'll probably be asked where I am. You won't know. You'll say that we drove together to the Cherry Bar and had a drink, and then I disappeared.'

'I suppose it could work,' said Lorna, 'But you've forgotten one little thing.'

'What little thing?'

'That Celia probably won't play the game the way you want it.'

'If life were all smooth, where would the fun be?' asked Mannering. 'If it works, telephone Larraby at his usual hotel, and ask him to go to the village, and keep watch.'

Lorna nodded.

The bedroom door opened, and Celia came out. She wore the mink coat, and a light hood edged with fur.

* * *

Mrs. Fleming was still unconscious. Mannering had warned Celia that she might be. Celia stayed for twenty minutes, and when she left the room, much of the whipped up vitality seemed to have seeped out of her.

* * *

Mannering drew her towards Fleming's door, and she hesitated, and pulled against him.

'I want to go back now, please.'

'You shall, soon.'

'I don't want to see my father.'

'He's not here,' said Mannering. He opened the door, and she saw that only Lorna was in the room. She went in. The visit to her mother was obviously still vivid on her mind. She was depressed, she didn't want to stay.

'I'm glad you came for me, but I must get back now,' she said.

'Celia,' Mannering was almost sombre. 'How far would you go to help your mother?'

'I don't understand you. The doctors are looking after her, aren't they?'

'Did you notice the nurse?'

'I couldn't very well help noticing her!'

'You don't know she is a policewoman.'

'What do you mean?' Celia's voice was tense.

'Your mother is under constant surveillance. The police suspect that she killed Muriel Lee. They're hoping that each time she comes round, she may say something which will give the truth away.'

Celia cried: 'No!'

'That is why the nurse is there. Celia, do you know who killed Muriel?'

'No!'

'Your mother had the opportunity, and she has a record of—'

'Why should she kill her? *Why?*'

'I don't know,' said Mannering. 'I don't think she did. I believe that someone else killed her, and would like it to look as if your mother is guilty. I want to find out who that someone is, I want to get at the whole truth. I think it will be an ugly truth, when it comes to light. And I want your help.'

'There's nothing I can do,' she said, and

looked at him with torment in her eyes.

'But I think that there is.'

'I know nothing about it!'

'Paul does.'

She didn't answer, didn't deny that it might be true. She looked older by ten years.

'I want to talk to Paul, and I want you to be away from him for a few days. If he didn't do it—all right, things can go on as they are. But I think he will try to use you as an alibi. He can make you do exactly what he wants, Celia, when he's with you—and sometimes when he's away from you. I know that you hate the thought that he might have had anything to do with this, but if you don't find out for certain, you'll never have a minute's peace. You don't have much peace, now. I want you to leave London for a few days, and let me deal with Paul. What I'm asking you to do, is simply to let him fight this out on his own. You won't be asked to betray him or do anything to harm him. Do you understand?'

She said: 'Yes, I understand.'

'Will you come away?' asked Mannering.

CHAPTER TWENTY

CHLOE'S COTTAGE

Her eyes stared burningly at Mannering, and she began to breathe heavily; gaspingly. It was as if she were fighting against an influence which had sprung into the room, unseen but powerful. Mannering guessed at its nature. She was tempted to do what he suggested, feared that he was right about Paul, and yet couldn't bring herself to defy him.

Lorna watched, fascinated.

Mannering kept his gaze on the girl's eyes; as Paul so often did. He could see the signs of the deepening struggle, and could not guess what the outcome would be. If anything broke this tension, she would probably collapse, and refuse to come; she would rush back to Buckley Street and wait for the man.

Someone walked along the passage. He had a momentary fear that it might be Fleming.

The footsteps passed the door, and silence fell again.

Mannering said: 'Your mother is in grave danger, Celia.'

She opened her lips and moved her hands, but didn't speak. She turned and darted a single glance towards the door, as if she could see through the walls to the woman who lay unconscious only a few yards away. Then she swung round, and stretched out her hands towards Mannering.

'Yes, I'll come,' she gasped. 'I'll come.'

* * *

The danger was from the lights outside the hotel; but it had to be chanced. With her hair hidden beneath Lorna's silk scarf and her face turned towards the ground, Celia walked with him to the car. Mannering couldn't see the watching police, but knew they were there. He took the wheel, leaned across and slammed the door, Celia sitting silently by his side. He moved off, and as he turned the corner, saw a police car following. He settled down to plan the best way to shake it off, and told Celia what he was going to do. She made no comment. He drove at speed as far as Marble Arch. The police car was some distance away. In Oxford Street, he beat two sets of traffic lights, then turned to the right, pulling up in a cul-de-sac, near one of the Squares. An illuminated sign, with a bunch of cherries flashing on and off, spread a red glow over him and over Celia.

No one showed any interest in him or the car.

Ten minutes later, Lorna drove up in a hired Buick.

In two minutes, Mannering was driving the Buick, with his coat collar turned up and his hat pulled low over his forehead. Celia was wearing her mink again. He made for the Great West Road. The powerful car responded to every effort he asked from it, they touched ninety miles an hour along the main road itself, and then settled down to fifty miles an hour towards Winchester.

* * *

The headlights of the car shone upon the windows of the cottages in the high street of Haddon village, on thatch and mellow brick, on tiny gardens and briared hedges. Mannering followed Chittering's instructions carefully, turning left at a fork, then driving along a narrow country lane for several hundred yards. He pulled up sharply, peering at an inconspicuous sign which stated:

Rose Lane Cottage
District Nurse

'We're here,' he said.

He helped Celia out. She hadn't spoken since they had left London and now he half expected her to cry out in sudden protest, to wish that she hadn't come, to want to go back. But her calm remained unbroken.

There were lights on at two of the windows of the cottage.

He'd told Celia what he had arranged, and repeated the gist of it.

'You understand, don't you, that you're a friend of Miss Chittering's, staying with her for a few days. You haven't been well, and you're resting. You're not to leave the cottage, except with Jane Chittering or her friend Chloe, until I've been to see you again.'

'Yes, I understand,' she said.

Mannering started to walk with her along the gravel path, but she put her hand arrestingly on his arm.

'Why do you hate Paul?'

'I don't know him well enough to hate,' said Mannering. 'I do know him well enough to believe he'll do anything to get his own way, and that this time, he mustn't get it unless he's innocent. If he is—'

'He must be,' said Celia, with a note of

pleading.

'Then all will be well,' said Mannering.

There was an old-fashioned pull-type bell, which clanged noisily at his touch. Immediately there were sounds of movement inside, the door was flung open, and Chloe stood there, both hands out-stretched, Jane close behind her.

They drew Celia into a warm, pretty living room in which a log fire blazed.

Mannering left for Guildford, if not entirely relieved, yet with some of his anxiety ironed away.

Fleming had told him, quite freely, about his house. It was on the Horsham side of the county town, with several acres of ground, most of it planted with fruit trees. He also kept a few pigs, and had told Mannering that a neighbour had promised to look after them; there was no living-in servant. Mannering parked his car a hundred yards away, and then walked to the house, *Maylands*. There was no light, except from the stars.

He walked round the front garden, and then stood close to the black cavity of the front door, and watched the nearby road. There was no sign either of the house being watched or that he had been followed. The police might have been here, but he doubted whether they would have been able to get a search warrant. Nevertheless he waited patiently and in utter silence for ten minutes. When the cold began to creep into him, he turned to the door.

He was fully equipped for his enterprise, with cotton gloves, knife, and a scarf, which he could pull over his face in an emergency. Examining the lock, he found it to be a mortice, more difficult to force than a Yale, but having the advantage that it could be opened without damage. He left the porch and walked to the back of the house. Both fowl-house and pigsty were visible as humped shapes at the end of the garden, and by them was the garage. The walls of the house were cream-washed and he knew that if anyone looked this way, he might be seen.

There was a little porch over the back door.

He studied the lock. It was also a mortice, but easier than that at the front. The disadvantage of back door entry was that it was often bolted and chained when the house was empty.

He started on the lock with his knife.

Making a little noise was unimportant, and enabled him to work faster. The lock clicked back. Feeling the usual quiver of excitement, but keeping it well in control, he pushed the door—and it opened.

He stepped inside the pitch-black void, closing the door behind him. A streak of sky could be seen from one window. He pulled the curtain across, then switched on his torch.

This was a big, roomy kitchen, modernised and uncluttered. The door leading to the front of the house was closed but not locked. He stepped into a wide passage, and the torchlight shone on a rug, parquet flooring, and several oddments of good furniture.

He went into each of three downstairs rooms and drew the thick curtains; they were heavy and of excellent quality. Once they were drawn, he switched on a light in the front room. It was large, and extremely well furnished. Mrs. Fleming had good taste, and money had evidently not been spared. A baby grand stood in one corner, and on it were three photographs, two women and two men.

One was Celia, as a girl; the other of Fleming, his wife, and a younger, fair-haired man, with a touch, Mannering decided, of irresponsible charm.

He went upstairs.

There were five bedrooms, and all had the same good taste and evidence of money freely spent. In one room there was a bowl of daffodils, not yet faded. Why had Mrs. Fleming taken the trouble to leave flowers in a bedroom, when she had known that she would be away for several days?

There were clothes in the wardrobe, books on a table within reach of the bed, and he opened two of them. Both were inscribed: 'Celia Fleming'. So this was Celia's room, and the flowers were altar offerings to Celia. The room looked as if it were kept lovingly, further evidence of the attachment between mother and daughter. Celia's hatred was centred on her father; as she had shown from the beginning.

He glanced into all the bedrooms, then went downstairs. The smallest room was a study cum library, with the walls by the fireplace lined with books. There were several large photographs showing Fleming in the saddle, dressed for polo. Others had obviously been taken in India. There was a small, old-fashioned safe.

Mannering opened it with swift, single-minded skill.

Inside were a few personal oddments of jewellery, bank pass books showing a total balance of three thousand pounds, twenty-five pounds in one-pound notes, account books, deeds of this and two other houses—all the things one might expect to find, but nothing about Celia, Smith or Muriel Lee. He closed and locked the safe; so far, he had done nothing which would betray the fact that anyone had searched here. He examined the bookcases, looking for concealed hiding places, and found none. The books, he noticed, were fairly general, but mostly travel and biography.

He searched the other downstairs rooms, and found nothing which confirmed or denied Fleming's story. He went upstairs again, but when he had been inside the house for an hour, he was convinced that there was nothing here to incriminate Fleming— nothing that suggested a motive for the murder of Muriel Lee, nothing to indicate his relationship with Smith.

Mannering felt disappointed but not dissatisfied. He'd wanted to check on these things, no one need know that he had ever been here. In an hour's time, he could be back in London.

He went through the house again, lingering only at the door of Celia's room. He left all the doors as he had found them, then did the same downstairs. He would leave by the back door, locking it behind him. Professionally he had done a good job, even if the results were negative.

The deep burr of a car engine broke the silence.

He was in the kitchen when he heard the car draw up outside.

CHAPTER TWENTY-ONE

NIGHT VISIT

He heard the slam of the car door as he was about to escape.

If he went out now, he would have no time to re-fix the lock; if the house were found unlocked, an alarm would immediately be raised. He closed the door and started to work on it. The scraping of metal on metal seemed loud. He wasn't sure whether the caller was coming at the front or the back of the house, but as yet had heard no sound of the front door opening.

Footsteps approached.

The lock turned.

Mannering switched off his torch and backed towards a recess under the stairs, filled with hanging coats. It was the only hiding place. He pulled a coat in front of him as he heard the key scraping in the lock. The door opened, and a man stepped in. A light went on, shining brightly into the hall passage. Mannering, pressed into the corner, was unlikely to be seen at a casual glance. A shadow appeared, followed by a tall man, who was past Mannering in a flash; Mannering had an impression of an attractive face and a hat on the back of a young, fair head.

A door opened and another light went on; the man knew his way about. Glass clinked; so he was pouring himself out a drink.

There were other sounds, faintly blurred, as if he were sitting down. It was nearly two o'clock in the morning, most men would make straight for bed, if they lived there; but this man didn't. Fleming had been definite that the house had been shut up. Mannering moved from his hiding place. The light was on in the front room, the door ajar. He stepped cautiously towards it, and was able to see through the crack between door and wall. The man was sitting back in an easy chair, as if he were thoroughly at home, and the drink was by his side. His expression was contented, almost smiling; it was hard to believe that he didn't belong here.

Then he took something out of his pocket. It caught the light, and Mannering saw that it was a key. The man bent over the side of the chair and picked up a small brief-case. He unlocked this, and took out a wad of one pound notes. Slapping the notes against his palm, in a gesture of self-congratulation he laid them on the arm of his chair, and drew out two further packs; Mannering judged that there were two hundred and fifty notes in each. Two more followed. Voluptuously the man drew others from the briefcase. There were eight packets in all; two thousand pounds, if Mannering's guess was right.

'That ought to do,' he said.

He sipped his drink.

'It will have to do.' His voice was rougher, bravado touched with uneasiness, as if an ugly thought had entered his mind. Then he fell silent. Unmoving, Mannering studied him carefully. He was in the early thirties, attractive, in a boyish, untidy way. He didn't look like either of the Fleming's, but his photograph was on the piano. He picked up the notes and began to put them back in the briefcase.

He stopped abruptly, and raised his head. For a moment it looked as if he were staring straight at Mannering. Mannering backed with infinite caution—then heard what had made the other glance up; it was the throb of a car engine.

The sound became louder. There was now no doubt that the car was coming along this road.

The man put the notes away hurriedly, locked the briefcase, stood up and walked across the room. Without waiting to see where he put the notes, Mannering backed swiftly to his hiding place beneath the stairs.

The car drew up, a door slammed, and footsteps sounded on the front drive. Another light came on, that at the front door. The young man's shadow appeared again, but he didn't come towards Mannering.

There was a ring at the front door bell; next moment, the door opened.

Mannering heard nothing for the next two seconds, but could imagine two men standing and staring at each other. Then one of them spoke.

'Well, George, aren't you going to ask me in?'

The second arrival was Smith.

★ ★ ★

There were footsteps, and the door closed. The man called George hadn't yet spoken. A sound that might have been a subdued laugh, from Smith, travelled along the hall-way. Then the men went into the front room.

'Well, well, whisky already poured out,' Smith said. 'You must have expected me.'

'I didn't.' George's voice was hard, he was no longer contented and self-congratulatory.

'What the hell do you want?'

'Strange question to ask,' said Smith smoothly. 'May I help myself, it's a cold night?'

'Do what you damned well like.'

'That,' said Smith, 'is exactly what I propose to do. I haven't changed.' There was a pause, and then he went on: 'The Major keeps the right stuff. Well, George, where is she?'

George didn't answer.

'You mustn't try to fool me, you know,' Smith said, and although his voice was light, there was a touch of menace. 'I'm wide, George. I know you've got Celia. Where is she?'

'You must be crazy!'

'Oh, no.' The note of menace was more pronounced now. 'I'm not crazy, George, but you are. What made you think that a lounge lizard like Mannering could get the better of me? Where is she?'

'Don't you know?' asked George. He sounded bemused.

'No,' said Smith, 'I do not, but I soon shall.' He laughed; and there was another sound, a gasp, and then a thud; as if a chair had fallen. In the following silence, Smith laughed again. 'Did that hurt? Nothing like so much as the next one will, if you don't tell me where you've taken Celia.'

'I don't know anything about Celia!'

'That's what Mannering told you to say,' said Smith. 'I'm not green. Fleming persuaded Mannering to help him, Mannering got this bright idea, which coincided with yours. As you're back in England, you certainly know all about it.'

'I don't even know who you are talking about!'

'Don't you?' asked Smith. 'You'll learn.'

There was a pause; Mannering could imagine a blow being driven into George's face. He heard a scuffle but no gasp; the scuffling went on. Mannering groped among the coats, found a big raincoat and put it on over his own, pulled a Trilby hat over his forehead, wound his scarf round his mouth and nose, and went forward. The men were by the piano, struggling, pressed close to each other. Smith's back was to Mannering. He also saw George's hands gripping Smith's neck. The fingers were tight at first, then gradually relaxed. Suddenly Smith brought up his right knee. George gasped with pain and banged back, against the piano; it gave out a clanging discord, which hung lingeringly on the air.

Smith backed away; and Mannering saw a gun in his right hand.

'See this?' asked Smith, in that mock friendly voice.

George tightened his lips.

'It is a lethal weapon.' Smith said. 'It belongs to the Major. Aren't I careful? It has his finger prints on, too. At least, it hasn't got mine, and as I had it stolen from him this afternoon, presumably he's handled it lately. Any idea how long prints last on the handle of a gun, George?'

George muttered: 'Get to hell out of here.'

'But you don't understand,' said Smith. 'Either you will tell me where to find Celia, or I shall shoot you. It's a lonely country house, no one is likely to hear the shot, and it's the Major's gun. He will be in a spot then, won't he? Especially as I telephoned him, a couple of hours ago, and arranged to meet him. If you're found killed with his gun, the police might just manage to make four out of two and two, don't you think?'

George didn't speak.

Smith said softly: 'I'm not going to waste time, George. Where is Celia?'

His body hid George from Mannering's sight. He was quite confident that the house was empty, and didn't trouble to look round. He held the gun in front of him, and Mannering couldn't see that either; but he was sure that Smith meant to carry out his threat.

'*Where is Celia?*' Smith asked, still softly. 'If you don't tell me—out you go.'

George stood up. Mannering could just see his face. He was still pale, but there was no desperation in his eyes.

'You can do what you like, I can't tell you what I do not know. Who's this Mannering, by the way?'

'You know very well. I'll give you one more chance, George. Remember I don't particularly want you alive. You're a serious distraction. You and Muriel were always fools. And when you fell in love with Celia you made yourself more of a nuisance than ever. You're a menace to me, too—you could give too much away. Hurry, George. Where's Celia?'

Mannering took out his cigarette case, and stepped forward. There was tense silence in the other room. George believed that he would be shot, but was too far away to get the gun out of the other's hand.

Mannering reached the doorway, crouching, hidden from George. He raised the case, and then tossed it—not viciously but casually. It rose just above Smith's head, and George must have seen it, for he exclaimed. Smith didn't move.

'You can't fool—' he began.

The cigarette case dropped on to his head. He staggered, taken completely by surprise. All Mannering saw next was a flurry of movement from George, and then he heard the impact of a fist on Smith's face.

The gun fell.

George leapt at Smith, and there was murder in his eyes. He smashed at the man's face. He smashed again, and as Smith tried to fend him off, gripped his neck and began to squeeze. Mannering watched, seeing the fear of death come into Smith's eyes, and Smith's mouth gradually opening.

Mannering picked up the gun, held it by the barrel, and struck George on the temple. The blow was sharp enough to make him relax his grip, and sway to one side.

George muttered: 'Who—'

Mannering went forward, gripped Smith's coat by the lapels and dragged him to his feet; all Smith could see was the scarf and the Trilby hat. Mannering spun him round, and struck him, much harder than he had struck George. Smith's knees bent beneath him, and he fell. There was no pretence, he was knocked cold.

Mannering picked up his case.

'Who *are* you?' breathed George.

'You know he would have shot you, don't you?'

George nodded, dazed by the march of events.

'That's one life you owe me. Don't ask questions, just answer them. You're Muriel Lee's brother and you're fond of Celia Fleming. Right?'

'Yes.'

'You've been trying to get Celia away from Smith.'

'It's all I care about, nothing else matters.'

'Was your sister beginning to turn against Smith?'

'Why should I tell—'

'That life, remember? Was she?'

George Lee said: 'Yes, she's been turning against him for some time. He had a hell of an influence over her, but some of the things he's done upset her. We knew that if we could get Celia away for a few months, she'd probably snap back to normal.'

'And you were going to take her away?'

'Yes.'

'How?'

'Everything was fixed to get her out of the country. Muriel was going to tell Celia that Smith was in France, and had sent for her to join him. We've rented a little villa in Italy,

Celia loves the Italian Riviera. We believed we could persuade her to stay, once she was there. Getting her away was the trouble.'

'And Smith discovered this?'

'I didn't realise it—'

'Where have you been?'

'I've just come back from Italy.'

'Where did you get the money?'

'From Major Fleming.'

'So he's in this plot?'

'He doesn't know what we're going to do, only knows we're going to try something.'

'When did you get the money?'

'I—how the devil do you know about it?'

'I've been here for some time,' said Mannering, dryly.

Smith stirred. Mannering turned towards him and studied him dispassionately. He was still unconscious, but would soon come round. Mannering picked him up bodily and carried him through the hall into the kitchen. George Lee followed, dazed and uncertain.

'Get some cord or rope,' Mannering said briskly.

Lee obviously knew the place well, and found a knot of cord in a drawer. Mannering tied Smith's hands and feet, then sat him on a kitchen chair. Smith head was lolling to and fro, but his eyes were beginning to flicker.

Mannering turned and led the way out. His scarf slipped a little and he adjusted it; it muffled his voice and was hot and uncomfortable, but he had no wish that George should see him clearly.

George said: 'Who *are* you?'

'I work for a man called Mannering. Forget it. Where did you get two thousand pounds? When did Fleming give it to you?'

'It was in an old tool box in the garage—he used it as a safe,' said Lee.

'Why do you need two thousand pounds?'

'I've made arrangements for plenty of money to be placed at my disposal in France and Italy. I'm to pay this into my friend's account over here, he stipulated that it should be in cash.' George was anxious to talk freely and to convince. 'Look here, who are you? Does this Mannering know anything about Celia? Has she disappeared?'

'Yes,' said Mannering. 'She's all right.'

'You mean—'

'I mean that someone else had the bright idea that it might be a good thing to separate her from Smith,' said Mannering. 'She won't come to any harm. She probably knew that Muriel was planning something against Smith, didn't she?'

'She—she might have done.'

'That would explain it,' said Mannering, and smiled behind the scarf. It explained why Celia had been amenable, if she knew what Muriel had been planning, she would more readily believe that Smith had killed the girl. The murder of Muriel and Celia's behaviour were easy to understand now.

Lee said sharply: 'What do you mean? Explain what?'

'Why Muriel was murdered,' Mannering said.

Lee cried: *'Murdered!'* The word shrilled through the house, not loud, but vibrant with emotion. Before Mannering realised what he was going to do, Lee rushed forward, thrust him aside and pounded towards the kitchen like an avenging fury.

CHAPTER TWENTY-TWO

MAN ALIVE

Mannering reached the kitchen as Lee picked up a chair and raised it high above his head. There was murder in his face as he rushed at Smith. Smith's eyes were open, and he saw what was coming. He couldn't move his hands, couldn't do anything to save himself. The chair smashed downward as Mannering flung himself at Lee. They fell together and as Mannering, momentarily stunned, struggled to get up, he saw Lee standing behind Smith, with his hands round the man's neck.

Smith was straining forward in the chair, and his eyes were flaming with fear.

Mannering grabbed the chair; there wasn't a moment to lose. He banged Lee over the back of the shoulders. Lee didn't release his grip. Mannering struck him again, then gripped his wrists until Lee at last let go.

Mannering watched the younger man as Lee breathed gaspingly. It was easy to see that he wasn't for the moment, sane, but he made no further attack, and Mannering relaxed.

He put his hand up to his scarf, which in

the scuffle had dropped. Smith was looking at him, with dazed recognition. There was nothing Mannering could do about that now. He took off his hat and tossed it to a chair. Both Smith and Lee followed its flight, as if it had some hidden significance. He lit a cigarette, took it across and placed it between Smith's lips.

Lee was also lighting a cigarette, with trembling hands.

'That's two lives you owe me,' Mannering said. 'Two each. Enjoying yourself, Smith?'

Smith didn't answer.

'I've been here some time,' Mannering said. 'I followed Lee. He was silly enough to leave the back door unlocked.' That wasn't true, but Lee didn't deny it, and it might satisfy Smith about the ease with which he had got in. If Smith knew he had forced a lock, he would probably start thinking, and soon reach the mysterious Mr. Brown. He might be there already.

Smith grunted.

'And I heard an interesting conversation. I now know why you killed Muriel.'

'I agree as to the interest,' said Smith, 'but if you are taking up eavesdropping as a profession, it is unwise to believe all you hear.'

'You fixed it.' Mannering said steadily.

'Lee, I'm the Mannering Smith spoke about who is helping Major Fleming. I know where Celia is.'

'So you managed that one all by yourself,' said Smith, in mock admiration. 'One day, if you keep trying, you might think up something that's really original.'

'Such as what to do with a man who starts to kill another, with a third party's gun,' suggested Mannering. 'You might get away with framing Fleming on one job, you wouldn't succeed with two.'

'Wouldn't I? Nevertheless there's a certain opulence, a lack of niggardliness, about two that appeals to me. If I wanted to frame Fleming, I couldn't think of a better way than killing the Lees. The Flemings blame the Lees for Celia's fall from grace. Don't they think she's grown up yet?'

'They think she's had a bad break,' Mannering said.

Lee ground a half-smoked cigarette into an ash-tray. His voice was husky.

'What happened to Muriel?'

'She was killed in Fleming's hotel room, last night.'

'I'll get you for it, if it's the last thing I do,' Lee said, and his eyes were smouldering as he looked at Smith.

'I wasn't anywhere near the hotel last night.' Smith said righteously. 'Mannering and all the police in Scotland Yard couldn't prove that I was there. You may not believe it, Mannering, but I hadn't anything to do with Muriel's murder, though I would have thoroughly enjoyed killing George.'

'And framed Fleming.'

'Certainly.'

'What have you got against Fleming?'

'I just don't like him,' Smith said pleasantly. 'When are you going to take these cords away, Mannering?'

'I haven't decided what to do with you yet. It would make a pretty story for the police.'

'You won't take it to them.'

'Why not?'

Smith said: 'You haven't got what you want yet.'

'And what do you think I want?'

Smith grinned.

Lee said abruptly: 'I can't believe it. Muriel *dead*. Mannering don't trust him. He killed Muriel. He knew we were planning to take Celia away, and it was his method of stopping me.'

'Why did you work for him in the first place?'

Smith said approvingly: 'That's right, my

boy, answer that one.'

Lee flushed, but didn't avert his gaze.

'Muriel fell for him. I wanted to part them, but he offered me a good job. As Muriel said she was in love with him and wouldn't leave him, I took it. That was a long time ago. I've been in and out of the Army since then.'

'And you came back and worked for Smith?'

'Why not?'

'What work did you do?'

Smith interrupted with a practised smoothness: 'Honest work, Mannering! I've a legitimate business, didn't you know? George is a pretty good buyer. He buys up all the electrical appliances for me, mostly bankrupt stock, and then the mail ordering gets busy. As for Muriel, our affair was washed up years ago. At first George was pretty sore about the way he said I'd treated her; and then he met Celia. Believe it or not, dear George lost his heart.'

The words seemed to sear the air.

Lee said thickly: 'You fooled me for a long time, but I got wise to you. And from then on I planned to take both Celia and Muriel away from you. I would have done it, too, I would have done it.'

'Don't you believe it. If Mannering hadn't

come along, Celia wouldn't have left the flat. She wouldn't trust you as far as she could see you.'

'That's a lie! There was a time when—'

'She had a crush on you? Poor dear George. She was merely practising on you.'

Lee said: 'I can't stay in the room with this swine any longer, if I do I'll break his neck.' He blundered out, and they heard a door close with a bang.

Smith's lips curled.

'Don't trust him, Mannering.'

'I haven't reached the stage of trusting anyone.'

'You're wise. What about cutting these cords?'

'I'm still undecided,' Mannering said. He turned on his heel. Glancing back from the door, he saw venom in the man's expression, and in his eyes the unfamiliar emotion of fear.

It would do Smith no harm to endure for a while the treatment he was so prone to give to others.

Mannering went into the big room. George Lee was sitting in the armchair in which he had so contentedly counted the money. His explanation of that might be true; but—on the other hand—it might not. It was as well to remember that all good liars sounded plausible. Now Lee looked dejected and distressed, with a cigarette drooping from his lips, his eyes wide open and his gaze fixed on the ceiling. He didn't glance at Mannering, who went across to the cocktail cabinet, and poured out two whiskies and sodas. He needed one himself.

Lee shook his head.

'Don't be a fool,' said Mannering.

Lee took the glass, and sipped.

'I just can't believe it,' he said. 'I knew I'd live to regret getting mixed up with a swine like Smith, but that he should kill Muriel—' he tossed the drink down and pushed the glass away with an ungentle hand. 'Oh, *I've* asked for it. But Muriel was still in love with him. Only when I realised that he'd some damnable influence over her and over Celia, did I see how bad he is. He crawls. Did you know that he uses hypnotism?'

Mannering nodded.

'When Muriel and I discovered that, we knew how crazy we'd been. We tried to get Celia away. Now—I don't know what to do, she's dead—'

'Celia isn't.'

'Muriel could have done more with Celia than anyone else possibly can,' said Lee. 'I won't have a chance, myself, she never looks at any other men. Smith's got her exactly where he wants her. Muriel would have helped to get her back to normality and later—'

He stopped, and literally shook himself. His voice deepened. 'Oh, hell!'

He went out, but there was nothing wild about him this time. Somewhere nearby, water splashed vigorously out of a tap. Soon, Lee returned, his hair rough dried into points.

'That's a bit better.' He forced a grin. 'I've got to get a grip on myself. What are you going to do with Smith?'

'Let him go, but he doesn't realise it yet.'

'Sure that's wise? We could charge him with assault, couldn't we? If the police knew all about it, they'd probably send him down for a year or two. That would give Celia a real break.'

'She's having one.'

'Not while Smith's free,' Lee said.

'He doesn't know where she is, and she'll stay hidden quietly for a few days. In order to find her, he'll take big risks.'

Lee nodded, comprehendingly. 'Give him enough rope to hang himself. I suppose there's something in that. There's another thing you ought to know.'

'What is that?'

'He's in some racket or other. The mail order business at Buckley Street is just a blind. I don't know much about it, but just before I left England, Muriel told me she thought that he dealt in stolen jewels. She even said—' he broke off, and gave a forced laugh.

'Even said what?'

'That she thought he was the Shadow. You know, the chap who's making such a sensation. I don't think he'd have the guts but he might handle the Shadow's loot. Is that the kind of thing you hope to pin on him?'

'More or less,' said Mannering. 'Can you tell me anything more about Muriel's suspicions?'

Lee said: 'Sorry, no. I was obsessed with the need for getting Celia away. I didn't pay much attention. But I've had a lot of time for thought since. Too much. Been playing with the idea that we might catch Smith out on some crime. If he were jailed, it would give Celia a damned sight better chance.'

'Have you ever heard of a man called Caton?'

'Caton?' Lee frowned and pushed his fingers through his curly hair. 'No, I can't say I have. I knew a chap named Caton once, he was with my squadron for a few months. Should I know Caton?'

It could be an ingenuous reply; Mannering was inclined to think it an honest one. If it were honest, Lee had no idea that Smith was Caton.

'Did Muriel ever mention the name?'

'I don't recall it.'

'Where would Muriel's personal papers be—her Will, and all that kind of thing?'

'I doubt if she made a will, and she didn't have much in the way of private papers. They'd be at our flat—we shared a small flat, not far from Buckley Street.'

Lee's sad eyes showed a gleam of interest. 'You mean, she might have collected some dope on Smith, and kept it somewhere?'

'Possible. If they're at the flat, the police will have them. Why didn't you go straight there when you reached England?'

'Had a note from Muriel while I was away,' Lee said. 'I've got it somewhere.' He took out his wallet and began to rifle through its contents. 'She said that she thought the flat was being watched. That Smith was suspicious. And that he'd been asking for me and for information as to where I was. I thought he'd start throwing his weight about if I turned up there. I don't mind admitting that Smith puts the wind up me. He's an uncanny devil.'

'That's half pose. When did you arrange to come here?'

'I've been here quite a lot,' said Lee. 'I kept it secret—didn't want Smith to know. If he'd discovered that I was working with Major Fleming, he might have—'

He broke off, raising his hands. Some of the letters dropped.

'Might have done what?'

'It's hard to say.' Lee spoke sharply. 'The man just gets under my skin. If it hadn't been for Celia, we'd have had a head on crash a long time ago, but his influence over her—how the Devil did you manage to get her away?'

'There's a weak link in his influence—she's very fond of her mother.'

'Yes, I know that. Well, you fixed it, that's the main thing. Where is she? I'd like to see her, if only to say hallo.'

'There's plenty of time for that,' said Mannering. 'Sure you don't know where Muriel might have kept papers?'

'Only at the flat.'

'Oh, well,' said Mannering resignedly. 'What are your plans for to-morrow morning?'

'I was going to hare up to town and put this

cash into my friend's bank. The sooner it's off my hands the better. He'll be advised when it's there, and will release the funds to me, in Italy. I'm a bit worried about it, if the exchange control people find out there'll be hell to pay, but if ever a thing was justified—'

'Worry that out with your conscience,' Mannering said, and smiled. 'I wouldn't let it weigh too heavily. The question now—how to scare the wits out of Smith?'

'Sure you won't turn him over to the police?'

'Not yet,' said Mannering.

'Pity, in a way,' Lee said, 'but you seem to know how to take care of yourself. I'd be turning cold by now, if you hadn't come along. One day—'

'Forget it.' Mannering stood up.

'Here's that letter from Muriel,' Lee said.

'Thanks—may I keep it?' Mannering put the letter into his pocket. 'Where will you stay in London? The flat?'

'No, I don't think so. The Lithom Hotel, Aldwych.'

'Telephone me to-morrow evening,' Mannering said, and gave Lee a card.

'Right!'

'You might give me a hand getting Smith to the car,' added Mannering.

'Where are you going to take him?'

'The less you know, the better it's likely to be for you,' Mannering said.

* * *

Smith didn't speak when they went into the kitchen. He looked tired and sombre. Mannering ignored him, went to a drawer and took out a clean tea towel, then went behind Smith and tied it over his mouth and nose. He knotted it securely, while Lee stood watching. Smith had been here for an hour, was probably stiff and uncomfortable. He grunted when Mannering helped him to his feet, but remained passive. Mannering and Lee lifted him, Lee taking his legs, as they moved cautiously out of the house. The darkness lent eeriness to the scene as they pushed Smith into the back of his own car. There was little sound.

'Good riddance to a rather nasty piece of work,' Lee said, loudly enough for Smith to hear.

Mannering chuckled.

He took the wheel and drove off. Lee was going to collect the Buick from the field, and keep it in the garage. Once Mannering reached the main road, he drove fast. There was no sound from the rear, he might have been alone in the car. He sped along the Kingston by-pass, and stopped at the London end of it, to light a cigarette. He kept the engine running, but it made only a gentle purring sound. There was no other traffic on the road. Mannering drew at his cigarette and seemed to have all the time in the world to spare. The dashboard clock in the powerful Chrysler pointed to half-past four.

The cigarette was half finished before Smith muttered something which Mannering couldn't hear; the tea-towel muffled his voice. Mannering made no comment. Smith spoke again, and Mannering turned and pulled the gag down, so that it lay round Smith's neck, like a scarf.

'Did you speak?'

'Damn you,' Smith said viciously.

'Is that all?'

'What are you going to do?' Smith hated asking the question, hated showing fear; but it was in him, now, and every minute was torment.

'I still haven't decided. You don't know any safe ways of disposing of a body, do you?'

'I—'

'You yourself always seem to leave them about rather untidily, so you're unlikely to have any really brilliant suggestions I fear.'

'What good will it do to kill me?'

'Take a load off several people's minds, and let Celia start living again,' Mannering said. 'I can think of a dozen good reasons for killing you.' He laughed. 'What's your other racket, Smith?'

'Never mind that! I'll pay you anything you ask if—'

'Too bad,' Mannering said. 'I've all the money I need.'

'What do you want?'

'To see you dead—hanged for preference, but the police might not be able to collect the evidence. What's you racket?'

There was silence.

'Oh, well,' said Mannering. He turned round, tossing his cigarette out of the window, and let in the clutch.

'Mannering!' Fear sounded harsh and raw in Smith's voice. 'I'm in several rackets. One of them would be profitable to you, I could put a lot of jewels in your way. Old stuff, too.'

'Thief or fence?'

'The stuff passes through my hands,' Smith said. 'I'm one of the biggest receivers in the game. I'd give you first choice, for Quinn's.'

'Quinn's doesn't deal in stolen stuff.'

Smith said: 'I don't know what the hell you're playing at Mannering.'

'I'm interested in your rackets.'

'I—'

'How much blackmailing have you been doing lately?'

'I suppose Fleming told you that I put the screw on him once,' Smith said sullenly. 'That's not my regular line, but I can squeeze—'

Mannering laughed.

Smith said: 'To hell with you!'

Mannering drove on. Smith could shout, if he thought it worth the risk. He didn't. Mannering glanced round at him. The blinds were down, and Smith sat staring straight ahead. He must know that they were now in London. He was eaten up with fear, but still fighting against showing it. Fleming had said that this man's one weakness was a pride that could brook no humiliation; that was probably true.

They reached the West End; and then the Adelphi. Mannering stopped the car.

'You're nearly home,' he said. 'Listen, Smith. I'm looking after Celia Fleming, and I don't want you poking around. I'm going to get you for Muriel Lee's murder. If necessary, I'll report to the Yard about what happened to-night. Lee and I, between us, can have you sent down for several years. You're in a jam. Understand?'

Smith said nothing, but the tenseness in his attitude betrayed that he was listening.

'I'm going to unfasten your feet, and then we'll go to your flat. You're going to show me round. I propose to search it for all the evidence I can find of your various rackets, and I'm going to take that evidence away with me. If you start any funny stuff, the dossier will go to the Yard. Understand?'

Smith muttered an unintelligible assent.

There seemed to be no one in Buckley Street, but that might mean that the Yard man watching the place was keeping out of sight. Mannering helped Smith out of the car, and supported the man to the front door. Smith could hardly stand, and was gritting his teeth against the pain which went through his legs now that the blood was freely circulating. Without speaking he handed over his keys.

Mannering shut the flat door behind them as Smith staggered to a chair and dropped into it. Leaving the inner door open so that Smith was under constant observation, Mannering went into the study and began work on the desk. One of the keys opened the safe; he pulled back the hinged lid.

This time it wasn't empty. Mannering pulled out two chamois leather bags, untied the string of one of them and shook the contents out. Diamonds, rubies, pearls, already taken out of their setting, lay before him. They made a shimmering heap at which Smith stared tensely.

'Not bad,' Mannering said. 'The Shadow's last haul, I believe.'

Smith muttered: 'Supposing I am the Shadow?'

'Still think there's doubt about it?' Mannering dropped the jewels back into the bag, and tossed it into the safe.

'Where do you keep your other stuff?'

'To hell with you!'

Mannering said: 'Listen. I have only to go out, leaving you bound and gagged, and tip the police off about this, and they'll be here in five minutes. You'd be in dock within a few hours, and in jail within six weeks. Don't make any mistake about that. Where do you keep your other stuff?'

Smith muttered: 'At the garage.'

'Where are the keys?'

'You've got them in your hand.'

'Where's the safe at the garage?'

'In the room opposite the stairs. It's built into the wall, behind a radiogram.'

'I'm going to have a look,' Mannering said. 'If there's any trouble, the police will be your next visitors.'

He went into the lounge. Smith, too unsteady on his legs to fight, allowed himself to be tied up again, then gagged. Mannering left him, fairly comfortable, this time, and went across to the other flat.

One of the keys opened the door.

Mrs. Morant was in a small bedroom, sleeping the heavy, rather pathetic sleep of the middle-aged. The key was on the inside of her door. Mannering took it out and locked her in, then went downstairs.

CHAPTER TWENTY-THREE

DOSSIER ON SMITH

No one appeared to be in Buckley Street, and Mannering wasn't followed.

London was waking up. A stream of taxis passed him as he neared Palling Street. He pulled up a hundred yards away, and walked the rest of the distance. The Palling Garage was closed, its frontage blank, and without lights.

He let himself in with a key, going straight to the room where, as Brown, he had visited Smith. He went to the window and opened it, and looked out. There was a wide sill, and not a long drop to a square of concrete below. At the far end of the square was a door leading to a service road. He left the window open but pulled the curtains, then switched on the light.

The safe was where Smith had said he would find it.

He examined it for tricks; electric current was the most likely danger. There was none. He opened it with Smith's keys. It was crammed with small books, there were five wash-leather bags, wads of five pound and one pound notes, packets of most European currencies, and at least five hundred ten dollar American bills. He put all these aside. Behind them were two automatics, and several passports, each bearing Smith's photograph, under different names. Two of them bore unrecognisable photographs, probably of Smith in disguise. The man had prepared every possible escape route.

There was at least ten thousand pounds in the safe, apart from the jewels.

Mannering glanced at one bag of these; they were the results of the Shadow's recent hauls.

He looked through the books, and found one with a list of names and addresses, all of them in France, Italy, Belgium or Holland. In another book there were entries, showing the money which had been received from people overseas. The book purported to be a record of the transactions of the Mail Order business, and the sums quoted were small. Mannering found some pencilled figures on a slip of paper, and compared them with the last entries in the book. The trick entries were simple; if Smith received a thousand pounds from someone in Holland, it was entered as ten pounds. If the police ever queried his business dealings with the overseas people, he had a plausible answer.

Against most of the entries were letters. M appeared several times, C occasionally, and there were others. He guessed that these identified the messengers who had taken the stuff abroad. He looked at the labels on the chamois leather bags; each had an address abroad, and obviously these were to be taken out of the country. None was in Paris; apparently Celia wasn't to have gone to Paris as an envoy.

Were the jewels taken out of England like this? The risk at customs was big, but—

He needn't worry himself about that.

There were legal documents, deeds of houses and business properties; Smith was a wealthy man. There were several bank statements in different names, each showing high credit balances. One bundle of share certificates showed that under different names, he had big holdings in many gilt-edged stocks and in most of the good industrials. It was all carefully and cunningly done, but Smith had made one big mistake; leaving the stuff here.

It had to be left somewhere. But why hadn't he dispersed it?

Over confidence might be one of his faults,

too.

Mannering finished the search. At his feet was evidence which would send Smith to jail for ten years, but there was nothing about Muriel; nothing to associate him with murder; nothing about the Flemings or Celia.

The wise thing might be to telephone the police. If Smith were inside for ten years, Celia's troubles would be over. But there was more to it than that. Was Smith the Shadow? The only evidence here was that he handled much of the Shadow's takings.

Bristow had suggested that there might be several men, working to give the impression that there was only one Smith wanted 'Brown' to help. The impression that the Shadow did everything himself and kept aloof from others, was beginning to fade.

There was nothing in the papers, as far as he could see, to incriminate anyone else. Supposing Smith had several screws who could do a slick safe-breaking job—what would happen if he were caught? At the ring-leader's arrest, the gang would break up, but it wouldn't stop the activities of the others. It wasn't even certain that here were several men; he was anxious to find that out.

He went through the books and papers again. Some he put back into the safe. Others, he slipped into the manuscript pocket of his coat. The bank accounts, the share certificates and title deeds didn't greatly matter, but he kept a list, which was attached to each bundle, giving a summary of Smith's holdings.

He put the jewels back in the safe.

Satisfied that he'd returned nothing which might be helpful, he closed and locked the safe. As he straightened up, he glanced at the window, and he saw the curtains billow slightly, as from a sudden gust of wind; or from a draught.

He straightened up, and glanced over his shoulder.

The door was opening slowly.

* * *

He went across to the window. The curtains still moved in the draught created by the opening door. He made little sound and showed no sign of haste. He pulled the curtain aside, and looked out. At the end of the yard, by the gate in the wall stood a heavily built man whom he recognised. He let the curtain fall, and strolled to that part of the room which was out of sight of the door. The man outside was still cautious. Mannering began the sporadic whistling of a man at ease, as he looked round for a weapon. He could have taken one of the guns out of the safe, three minutes before; it was too late, now. He had his knife; and wished he had the cosh.

There was no fireplace and no poker, but behind a chair was a set of golf clubs. He took out a driver, whippy and light.

The door creaked.

Mannering, creeping towards it, noticed that it was now open a foot. He couldn't see who was beyond it.

Then suddenly the door flung back, and the little man who had admitted 'Brown' darted into the room. He seemed to expect assault, and had a walking stick in his hand. He saw Mannering, with the golf club raised, and stood, without speaking, his teeth bared and his eyes glistening.

'Hallo,' said Mannering. 'Something the matter?'

'Hallo to you,' said Smith.

He had a gun in his hand, as he came in.

* * *

Mannering backed slowly, still holding the club. Smith grinned at him, his poise fully restored. The little man having done his part by distracting Mannering's attention, glanced at Smith, as if awaiting orders.

'May I have my keys back?' Smith asked, suavely.

Mannering put his hand to his pocket, watching the gun. Smith's long, pale forefinger was on the trigger, and there was little doubt that he would shoot.

Mannering said: 'Whose gun have you borrowed this time?'

'Now it's my turn to ask the questions,' Smith said.

Mannering threw the keys, and Smith caught them with his free hand. He tossed them to his henchman.

'See what he's taken, Mick.'

Mick grabbed the keys and turned to the safe.

'Who let you out?' asked Mannering mildly. 'I locked Mrs. Morant in.'

'You forget she had a telephone in her room.'

'Oh,' said Mannering. 'The simple things.'

'That's right.'

Smith laughed; he was right back to normal, seemed thoroughly pleased with himself. He didn't look away from Mannering, who continued to grip the golf club, knowing it wouldn't be much use against a gun. Mick was taking things out of the safe and spilling them onto the floor; as yet, he hadn't checked on what was missing.

Suddenly a roaring sound shattered the quiet. It came from the garage, an engine turning on a high pitched note.

Smith's grin widened. He pitched his voice high, to be heard above the sound.

'Not bad, is it, Mannering? That's to prevent anyone from hearing the shot.'

The gun covered Mannering's stomach. Mick had emptied the safe, and was saying something that Mannering couldn't catch. Smith went across to him. Mick straightened up, holding one of the guns while Smith inspected the books and bags. He didn't take long. The whining note of the engine in the garage began to get on Mannering's nerves; the room seemed to shake with the reverberations.

Smith wasn't smiling now.

He came across to Mannering, standing so that Mick could keep Mannering covered. He shot out his left hand, and struck Mannering across the face; as he had once struck Celia.

'Now I'll have the stuff back,' Smith said.

'You can't very well,' said Mannering pleasantly. 'It's gone.'

'Don't lie.'

Mannering shrugged.

'Don't *lie*,' Smith said again. 'Where is it?'

'Safe enough,' Mannering said.

Smith's high-pitched voice had a deadly note. The gun raised, covered Mannering's face. 'I'm not going to waste any time, Mannering. Hand over those papers, or—'

'Too bad,' said Mannering. 'Don't forget you owe me a life.'

'I don't always pay my debts.'

'I was afraid of that,' said Mannering. 'What are you going to do when the police arrive?'

He strained his voice to make sure that Mick heard that; and smiled faintly as he finished. Mick's eyes shifted uneasily. Smith wasn't so sure of himself, either. His usual expression, the sardonic Mephistophelian half-smile, was worn with a certain amount of deliberation.

'You can't bluff—'

'No bluff,' Mannering said. 'I've the papers all right, they're in my pocket. I am not the only one, apparently, who forgets that there's a telephone. I called the Yard, just before you came in.'

'Now I know you're lying. They'd be here if you had.'

'I asked Bristow himself to come,' said

Mannering, 'and he won't be alone. You've about ten minutes, I should say.' He took out his watch with an air of nonchalance. Two guns covered him; and his only hope was to bluff.

'I don't believe you.'

Mannering shrugged. 'Just supposing they come, Smith. You may have time to hide the body, but you probably won't. Bristow's a wise old bird, and the garage is almost certainly being watched. You can't take me away safely. When he finds I'm missing, he won't be satisfied to look through the house, he'll search the garage. Call it a day.' He moved towards the door, and both guns swivelled round towards him. He was only a yard from the door, and it was open.

'Don't go any further,' Smith warned.

'Listen,' said Mannering, 'Bristow's a friend of mine, he knows I wouldn't call him out at this hour for the fun of it. You're stymied.' He raised the golf club, actually made a playful drive. 'Too whippy, and a bit long for me,' he said. 'What's your handicap?'

'Just stay where you are,' Smith said. 'I'm very patient. I'll wait for your friend Bristow, and if he doesn't come, I shall know what to do with the corpse.'

Mannering made another playful drive.

'If Bristow does arrive and you've still got the stuff in that safe, what do you think he'll do? Touch his hat and apologise for troubling you?'

He swung for another drive—and this time let the club fly out of his hands. As it went, he jumped towards the door. He caught the edge as he went through and slammed it behind him. There was no time to lock it. He reached the head of the stairs as the door reopened, flung his cigarette case at Smith, who was in front, and raced down the stairs. A shot rang out, just audible above the roar from next door; he heard the sound as it hit the wall close by his head. The front door was closed, he really hadn't a chance; unless they decided that he'd told the truth. He heard Mick say something. He didn't look round, but wrenched open the door; and nothing happened.

He dashed out.

The street seemed empty, but a man appeared from the garage; the man who had been on guard at the back of the yard.

CHAPTER TWENTY-FOUR

VISITORS

The man carried a big tyre lever in his right hand. He knew nothing of what had happened upstairs; he could smash Mannering's skull with that lever. They were only a couple of yards apart, and the big man's eyes were vicious and bloodshot. He raised his arm—and Mannering kicked out at him, caught him on the knee, and raced past.

The dynamo kept shrieking.

Mannering reached the end of the street, and slowed down. The big man was following, but several people were walking along here, and an open lorry trundled towards him. Mannering waited until it was level, then took a running jump on to the back. He barked his knee on the tailboard, but kept a hold. His pursuer turned the corner, lever in hand, but didn't see him. The lorry passed the end of Palling Street.

Smith was standing by the garage door. He moved back towards the house. Mannering waited until the lorry turned a corner, then slid off. Two people noticed him, and a man called out:

'No hanging on behind, there!'

Mannering waved.

He took the next turning which led towards Southwark Road. Now that the crisis was past, he felt overwhelmingly tired. He walked to the opposite pavement and waited with two or three shivering people for the next tram. He was exhausted; that probably accounted for his shivery feeling. He was elated, too, though fully aware that Smith hadn't shot his last bolt.

He got off on the other side of the bridge, had a cup of hot tea and a sandwich at a snack bar, then walked until he stopped an empty taxi. He went to Larraby's hotel, obtained some paper and string, and parcelled everything he had taken from the garage and asked the porter to post it to the G.P.O. Victoria.

It was a little after seven o'clock when, observed by Bristow's watching men, he let himself into his flat.

★ ★ ★

Lorna was asleep.

She hadn't undressed, just thrown herself down and pulled the eiderdown over her. One arm lying over the side of the bed, and one stockinged foot showed beneath the cover. He could imagine, with a pang half tender, half irritable, that she had waited in a continual strain of anxiety, that she hadn't undressed, in case he sent an S.O.S. There was no telling what time she had dropped off.

He lay and watched her for some time, and his eyes grew heavier and heavier. He didn't want to wake her, and yet he wanted to tell her what had happened.

He closed his eyes.

He had no idea what time it was when he woke, but he heard voices; someone was laughing, too. He lay in a dream-like state between waking and sleeping. It was broad daylight; of course it was, it had been daylight when he had reached home. He thought that Lorna was talking, was sure that the laughing man wasn't Bristow; but it was a familiar laugh.

He looked at the bedside clock; it was nearly half-past one.

He sat up.

The door began to open. *'Be quiet!'* Lorna whispered to whoever was with her, and then she turned and saw that he was awake. She closed the door and tiptoed across. He held out his hands, and she caught them tightly.

'Any trouble?'

'Not to say trouble.'

'Can you prove where you were between eleven and twelve last night?'

He frowned. 'Why?'

'Can you?'

'I left Chloe's cottage about half-past ten.'

Lorna sat heavily on the side of the bed.

'So you couldn't have been in London before twelve. Not to have—' she broke off, as the door opened, and Chittering stood there. 'I told you not to come in!' She jumped up.

'Sorry.' Chittering sauntered across the room. 'I had to see what the great man was like when he first woke up, and having fox's ears, I heard the whispering. Any alibi, John?'

'If Chloe and Jane make one, yes.'

'That's a relief.' Chittering tossed a copy of the *Record* on the bed. 'You can read all about the Shadow's latest burglary, discovered at five past twelve. The Shadow's bed time is getting earlier.'

Mannering didn't speak.

Lorna said: 'John, what is it?'

'Could it be a guilty conscience after all?' asked Chittering lightly.

Mannering patted Lorna's hand, absently, his thoughts whirling. If the Shadow had been busy between eleven and twelve o'clock, the Shadow wasn't likely to be Smith. He didn't think there was a chance that Smith would have broken into a Mayfair house last night, after discovering that Celia was missing.

'How I love strong, silent men,' said Chittering brightly.

'You could imitate them,' Lorna suggested. 'Are you going to get up now, John?'

'Yes. Chitty—how long were you with Paul Smith last night?'

'I wondered when you would come to that. I left him at a quarter past ten. He could have had time to do the job, I suppose? Just?'

'He was at Guildford soon after, and before that, he tried to find out what had happened to Celia. No, if the Shadow was out last night, Smith isn't the Shadow. Pity. That puts us back where we started. Has Bristow been?'

'Not yet.'

'A pleasure yet to come,' said Chittering sententiously. 'Have any luck last night, John, apart from parking Celia?'

'Odds and ends,' Mannering said. 'Well, we needn't worry about Bristow, that's a relief. What about lunch. . . .'

* * *

Bristow came just after three o'clock, appeared to be satisfied with Mannering's statement, and went off. Mannering telephoned the cottage. Jane and Celia were in; Celia seemed contented enough. He called George Lee, who said he had deposited the money, and had had a few hours sleep. He would stay at the hotel for the rest of the afternoon; he sounded sleepy. Mannering put the receiver down and looked across at the Rubens, which was still resting on a chair, identified now by all except the experts who mattered. But Mannering wasn't thinking about pictures.

Smith, then, *wasn't* the Shadow.

George Lee had a lot of money and had told a plausible story, but had he been out of England for the past few weeks? Or had he lied? There was still a lot to find out about George Lee and about the Shadow. Except that Mannering had discovered how the Shadow sold his pickings, he was no nearer solving his identity. Bristow's theory of three or four men couldn't be discarded, and if that theory now had substantial grounds for being right, it meant that Bristow no longer seriously suspected Mannering.

He picked up the telephone and asked for Toby Plender's number.

'I tried to get you this morning, but Lorna

wouldn't wake you,' Plender said.

'Sorry, Toby. Have you see Fleming?'

'I have indeed.'

'Is he a good liar?'

'If he's a liar he's the best I've met so far.'

'So you're satisfied that he told the truth?'

'I think so. His wife's come round, and she's confirmed part of it. I had a chat with her. The police have withdrawn the nurse, by the way. A little persuasion convinced Bristow that he was going further than the circumstances warranted.'

'Good work! Like another little job?'

'I suppose I'd better say yes,' said Toby.

'Thanks. I'm a little anxious to probe into the history of a Mr. George Lee, now at the Lithom Hotel, Aldwych. He says he's been on the Continent for several weeks. If you'd have a chat with him, and just get a general impression as to whether he's lying or not, I'd be grateful.'

'Distrusting your own judgment these days?' asked Plender.

'Second opinions add a certain flourish, especially when they coincide with one's own,' Mannering laughed, and rang off. He stared at the Rubens again. It was a brilliant job; one of the best, although it would probably take the experts months to agree. As he leaned forward for a further inspection, the telephone bell rang.

'Mannering here.'

Sylvester's voice travelled thinly across the wire. 'I'm sorry to worry you Mr. Mannering, but a certain Mr. Smith called at Quinns to see you about an hour ago, and was most insistent, almost embarrassingly so. He seemed a somewhat—ah—mysterious individual, and left a strange message.'

Mannering's hand was tight on the telephone.

'Yes?'

'He said that the lady's parcel must be sent to Paris and the smaller one returned to its owner, and that you would understand what he meant.'

Mannering relaxed. 'Thanks, Sylvester. Is there anything else?'

'Nothing requiring your personal and immediate attention,' said Sylvester. 'Goodbye, sir.'

Smith wouldn't expect him to take the message seriously; it was only the opening move in the battle of wits. It would be a desperate battle, for Smith would risk everything to get those papers back.

Someone came to the front door, and after a pause, Hetty approached the study. As she opened the door, Mannering saw Smith following quickly behind her.

* * *

Hetty said coldly: 'It's that man.'

'So you haven't forgotten me,' said Smith, and put a hand on her shoulder. She drew away with all the hauteur of outraged stage aristocracy, confronted with impertinence. Smith smiled fleetingly.

'Did you get my message, Mannering?'

'I stopped delivering parcels some time ago,' Mannering said pleasantly.

'I should start again, just for these two. You may think you've got me where you want me, but you'll find that that assumption is a mistake. I wonder where you keep the papers.' His gaze roamed round the room, and came finally to rest on Mannering. 'You didn't send for Bristow, you know, nor did the police turn up. That means that you're playing a dangerous game of your own. It also means that you don't confide in the police about everything. I wonder why.'

'Keep wondering,' Mannering said.

'I shan't, for long. I want Celia sent to Paris and the papers delivered to the garage by midnight to-night. If I haven't heard that both are safe—' he stretched out his hand and put his thumb towards the floor.

Mannering said mildly: 'I'll come for you when I want you, Shadow.'

Smith shrugged and turned away. Mannering watched him until the door closed. It made hardly a sound, but an uproar of voices followed. Mannering heard a stifled cry and the thud of a falling body. He reached the door and pulled it open. Major Fleming stood at the top of the stairs, and Smith, on his knees, sprawled on the landing below.

Fleming turned.

'Hallo, Mannering. I'm sorry I've used your landing as a summary court of justice. Can you spare me a few minutes?'

CHAPTER TWENTY-FIVE

'MR. BROWN' AGAIN

'You're a pretty useful man with your fists,' Mannering said, as he led the way into the study. 'Smith can give you ten years or more. How did you manage to throw him downstairs?'

Fleming shrugged.

'I keep pretty fit and know a trick or two. I didn't spend three years in the Burmese jungle for nothing. If I could deal with Smith with these—' he stretched out his hands with the fingers spread wide—'I'd be a happy man. What was he doing here?'

'Breathing fire.'

'I think he's beginning to get a healthy respect for you,' said Fleming.

'I wish you'd share it.'

Fleming frowned. 'Believe me, I do. Any man who can put the best barrister in England on to me, as you did, is worthy of anyone's respect.'

'Why didn't you tell me about George Lee?'

'That's what I've come to see you about.' Fleming was bland. 'I might also ask what you were doing at *Maylands* last night, but I'll assume that you had a good reason. I don't give a damn what you do, as long as I see Smith confounded and Celia free. I'll work with any man who'll help. George will do his best for Celia, there's no doubt about that. He and Muriel together might have succeeded. If you're going to ask me why I didn't tell you about Muriel's plot—' he shrugged his shoulders. 'It was obvious that it wouldn't come off, after her death. George couldn't do anything by himself. So I didn't tell you. In any case, I didn't expect him back until next week.'

'Did you leave two thousand pounds in a garage in the safe for him?'

'I certainly did.'

'Risky hiding place, wasn't it?'

'I've never known a better. I meant to slip home this morning and remove the money, as there was no further point in going on with George's bright idea, but—' he shrugged again. 'George is half-demented. He's begged me to let him take Celia away, saying it's the only hope for her, even now. I'm inclined to agree. Is it true that you know where she is?'

Mannering nodded.

'I did better than I knew when I came to you,' said Fleming warmly. 'How is she?'

'Right enough, and I think Smith's too busy to go after her. She's watched and in good hands. How's your wife?'

'Very poorly.' Fleming's shoulders drooped, as he slumped into a chair next to the Rubens. 'The nurse has gone, I've engaged a private one in her place. We shall stay at the hotel until my wife's fit enough to travel. That'll be the better part of a week, I suppose. Mannering—'

'Yes.'

'You know the police pretty well. Have they any idea of my wife's past record?'

'If they have, they've not informed me.'

'I'm still worried, in case they find it out and start thinking that she killed Muriel.'

'Did she know that Muriel was working with George to help Celia?'

'No. It would only have raised her hopes. With a woman whose mind is so finely balanced as my wife's, you have to be extremely careful. Why?'

'If she'd known, she wouldn't have had any motive to kill, would she?'

Fleming looked restlessly round the room, and his gaze fell on the Rubens. He appeared to study it. Without raising his head, he said: 'So you think she may have done it?'

'I'm trying to put myself into Bristow's

position. It's one of the factors to be taken into consideration.'

'Smith killed her. Or else he arranged for one of his men to do it. He surrounds himself with a bodyguard of criminals, and I think they'd do anything he ordered. Once the truth is known, my wife won't be in any danger. Until then, she'll be in a great deal. There's nothing I can do myself, but I'm relying on you, Mannering.'

'There may be a lot you can do yourself.'

'Such as?'

'Find out, at the hotel, whether any strangers were about on the night of the murder. Find out who arrived that day, and stayed only the one night. Try to check on the staff, see if they had anyone in temporarily that night.'

'Surely Bristow will see to all that?'

'But he won't tell me the results.'

'I see,' said Fleming. He turned away from the Rubens, without comment. 'I'll be glad to do what I can, and I'll tell you if there's any news. Is that all?'

'For the time being,' said Mannering. 'What's the relationship between George Lee and Celia?'

'I wouldn't say that there is one.'

'He thinks there is.'

'He's in love with her. It isn't the hardest thing for a man to fall in love with Celia.' Fleming's voice grew gentle. 'I think he's a good chap. He's a bit weak, and fell under Smith's domination for a time, but he's all right at heart. It's no use asking me whether Celia is interested in him—I just don't know. They didn't meet until after she'd gone to Smith.'

'How long have you known Lee?'

'About a year.'

'How long has this kidnapping plot been going on?'

'About four months. Until then, I'd only met Lee casually. Then he came to me, and we had a long talk. I jumped at the chance that he might do something to help Celia. You know the rest.'

'Is this the first time you've given him money?'

Fleming looked up sharply.

'What are you getting at?'

'Is it the first time?'

'Well, no. I've let him have a few hundred pounds, at intervals. He threw up his job with Smith, and hadn't anything much left. He couldn't get another job and do what he could for Celia, so I staked him. I thought it was a good investment. Have you any reason to think that he's not trustworthy?'

'It's one of the things we have to find out,' said Mannering.

★   ★   ★

After Fleming had gone, Mannering went up to the studio, to see Lorna. She was standing by the easel, looking critically at a wet landscape. Half finished canvasses were stacked in twos and threes, most of them facing the walls. Lorna's hair was untidy, and there was a dab of burnt Sienna on the side of her chin.

Mannering studied the picture.

'No opinion at this stage, please,' said Lorna. 'What have you done to Hetty? She was almost in tears when she brought me a cup of tea.'

'She doesn't like Smith.'

'I haven't seen him,' Lorna said, 'but already he makes me want to scream. John, must you go on with this?'

'Must you go on with that?' Mannering glanced at the landscape.

Lorna said dryly: 'The point is taken.'

'It can't go on much longer.' There was a note of appeal in Mannering's voice. 'Smith is feeling pretty vicious. It'll be a quick finish and a nasty one. Do you feel like enlisting the aid of the police?'

Lorna didn't speak.

'I'm serious. And I think Bristow would pay more attention just now to you than he would to me. Tell him that a new character has appeared, a George Lee, who worked for some time with Smith's mail order business, as a buyer. Ask him if he can find out anything about this Smith who's supposed to have been on the Continent a lot lately.'

'And why am I supposed to find that of burning interest?' inquired Lorna.

'Because you are worried that I am mixed up in it, and that he may not be trustworthy. Description—' Mannering took the photograph from inside his coat, and handed it to her.

'He looks a bit feckless,' Lorna said critically. 'What has he done, that you should hand him over to the police?'

Mannering said with the careful manner of one divulging a rather natty plot: 'It may give Bristow a good chance to be heavy-handed. You know the record: "I've told John a hundred times that he'll burn his fingers one of these days. This man is . . ."' Mannering broke off. 'If Lee's got a record, it'll give the job a new slant. He's so ingenuous that it's almost suspicious, and Bristow won't give me any help on a direct approach.'

'I'll see what I can do,' Lorna said at last.

'And also see if there's any news about Muriel Lee's murder. Bristow might drop you a hint.'

'What do you expect to hear?'

'That he's very suspicious of one of the Flemings.'

'And you aren't?'

Mannering kissed her lightly on the forehead, and went downstairs, without answering. He took the make-up case with him, and left the flat. His car was standing outside; Lee had arranged for it to be driven back. He drove straight to Trafalgar Square, without being followed. Why had Bristow taken his watch-dog away?

It was still broad daylight, a risky time for disguise. He went to the Post Office, and asked for letter to Mr. John Brown. There was one. Slipping it into his pocket he went outside and watched, to make sure that no one had observed him. Satisfied, he went back through the Post Office and out of the entrance opposite St. Martins-in-the-Fields. He could see no loitering figure. He went to his car and drove towards Piccadilly, stopping in Leicester Square to read the letter. The address was typewritten; so was the note inside, and there was no signature. But it was from Smith, who had written:

'I want to see you to-night. I've a job for you. No risks and it's worth two hundred pounds.'

Mannering flicked his lighter, lit the corner of the note and let it burn. He was smiling. But it was a strained smile.

If Smith had no idea of the connection between 'Brown' and Mannering, all might go well. If Smith guessed, or half-guessed, he would be walking into a trap. He didn't think that Smith would let him go again, unless—

There were so many possibilities, one of them highly dangerous. If Smith half-guessed the truth, he could have the grease paint off in five minutes—sufficient to recognise Mannering. Once he knew that Brown was Mannering, he would hold all the high cards. But 'Brown' might find out the truth about the murder, about the Shadow and about Smith, in a matter of hours. Lorna would say it was a crazy risk that wasn't justified.

'But if Smith was a public menace. . . .'

If Mannering went, he would have to go alone.

Larraby could have helped; but Larraby's job was important. Certainly Celia couldn't be left unguarded at the cottage.

It was a little after four o'clock.

He drove towards Fleet Street, reached the *Record* Office and found the big newsroom almost deserted. The fierce rush of work hadn't yet started, this was a recession period. Chittering wasn't there. He went across to the Red Lion and found the reporter in the tea room. Chittering sauntered across to him, leisurely.

'Got a story for me?'

'Maybe. Busy to-night?'

'I'm always busy.'

'Could you go and amuse Chloe for a while? I've a job for Larraby.'

'Won't I do?' Chittering was hopeful.

'Sorry, no.'

'Oh, well,' said Chittering. 'I can tell the Old Man that I'm on a hot job, I suppose it will be all right. Any objection to me interviewing the lovely Celia?'

'A very strong one, you're just the brother of your sister Jane.'

'The things I do for you,' said Chittering. 'I suppose it's a rush job.'

'If Larraby can be at Aldgate Station at seven o'clock to-night, I'll be happy,'

Mannering said.

'It'll mean breaking every speed limit invented by man. All right, John. I'll do what I can.'

★   ★   ★

Mannering telephoned the Palling Garage and left a message for Caton; that he could not arrive before seven thirty and might be later. The voice which answered was that of the little man who had burst into the room ahead of Smith earlier that morning. Mannering drove off, parked his car, then went by bus to the Edgware Road. He needed special make-up for tonight, and only Old Sol could do it.

At a little after six o'clock, Mannering looked at himself in a mirror, and marvelled. It was by far the best job that Old Sol had done on him. He went by bus to the house in Paddington, reaching there a little before seven o'clock.

The motherly woman told him that two men had called to see him; from the descriptions, they were Mick and the big man.

No one was in the street. Mannering walked back and at the nearest garage, hired a car, giving Old Sol as a reference. It was a roomy Austin, with a good turn of speed. He drove through the brightly lit streets to Aldgate, arriving soon after seven fifteen.

Larraby was standing in the entrance to the underground station, reading an *Evening News*. He glanced up as Mannering approached.

'How are tricks, Josh?'

Larraby lowered the paper. He looked intently at Mannering, but made no comment on his appearance.

'All well at the cottage?'

'I understand that Miss Fleming is quite content to stay there,' Larraby said.

'Good. Now listen, Josh. I'm going to the Palling Garage. I don't know whether Smith is pulling a fast one or not. He may suspect that Brown is Mannering. I want you to be at hand. I'll raise an alarm if there's trouble. If it gets through to you, telephone the police. And do the same if I'm not out within the hour. All clear?'

'Perfectly,' said Larraby. 'Shall we make separate ways to Southwark?'

'I'll give you a start. Go by taxi.'

'Very good,' said Larraby.

He drifted into the flow of pedestrians with intuitive skill. With time on his hands, Mannering turned to the telephone kiosks, and dialled his Chelsea number.

'Hallo, sweetheart.' Mannering's voice had laughter in it. 'How did you get on with the great detective?'

Lorna didn't answer.

'You there?' Mannering was anxious.

'Yes, I'm here,' said Lorna slowly. 'John, be very careful.'

'So George Lee's a bad 'un,' Mannering said.

'Bristow isn't certain. He's promised to check. He's pretty sure that it was Mrs. Fleming who killed Muriel. She was drunk, early in the evening, and he is fully aware of her past record.'

Mannering said: 'That's bad.'

'He's not sure whether Fleming knows. He thinks it's worth holding his hand for a day or two. He's taken his men away from River Walk, too—but he says you're in deeper waters than you realize. He didn't say so, but it was fairly obvious that he believes that Smith, the Shadow, Lee and the Flemings, are all involved in big crime.'

'And what else?' asked Mannering.

Lorna didn't answer at first; then she said evenly: 'I've just had a call from Chittering.'

Mannering's heart began to thump.

'And?'

'Smith's found Celia. He must have followed Chittering. Chittering and Chloe were with Celia at the cottage when he attacked them. Neither of them is badly hurt, but Smith took Celia.'

CHAPTER TWENTY-SIX

'MR. SMITH AND MR. BROWN'

Mannering left the car a short distance from Palling Street, and walked to the garage. The big man in his shirt-sleeves was working at a taxi, the nearside rear wheel of which was off. He didn't glance at Mannering. Larraby was at the end of the street; he showed himself long enough for Mannering to see him, and then disappeared; there was no need to worry about his hiding place; Josh would do his job well.

Mannering knocked at the door.

It was several minutes before Mick opened it. He peered at the newcomer, and then stood against the wall. There seemed to be a click of finality in the sound of the closing door. Mick hadn't yet said a word. Now he followed Mannering as he went slowly up the stairs.

He had an automatic in his pocket.

The door of Smith's room was closed. Mannering tapped on the panel. The radiogram could be heard, tuned low; the sound of operatic music came faintly into the room, Mick stepped inside after Mannering, closing the door. His pinched face was dark with suspicion.

There was insolence in Smith's manner as he sat back in his chair with studied nonchalance. Watching him, Mannering thought that Smith would behave like this if he were about to spring a trap. Mick stood by the door, openly making sure that Mannering couldn't get away. It was difficult to look unmoved into Smith's eyes, wondering whether they were piercing his disguise.

'What do you want?' Mannering demanded.

'You read my note. I've a special job. But before you get it, I want to be sure you can be trusted.'

'Why bother me, if you think I can't be?'

Smith grinned, his teeth white and even and cruel. He was different, more confident, than he had been at Chelsea. It was hard to believe that the last time Mannering had seen him he had been on his hands and knees, glaring with hatred at Fleming.

'I know a lot about you, Mr. Brown. The police would like to know where you live and what you do for a living, wouldn't they?'

Mannering said: 'I haven't come here to waste my time.'

'You're not wasting it. On the contrary, I

feel it's well invested, for I have a job for you. You're to get certain books and papers for me. I can tell you where they're likely to be. When you've found them, you're to bring them straight to me. The slightest delay and I shall telephone the police and tell them where you've been. Understand?'

'You can trust me,' Mannering muttered, his voice as off-hand as he could make it.

'Possibly, but I'm making quite sure. Have you heard of an antique shop, called *Quinns*?'

'Well, I seem to have,' Mannering said. 'It's in Mayfair isn't it?' He broke off, with deliberate hesitation. Smith was watching him closely; it was not improbable that the question was a trap.

'What's on your mind?' Smith growled.

'That's Mannering's place.'

'You a friend of Mannering?'

'Friend! Why, he's dangerous! He's as close as that with the police. It's asking for trouble.' Mannering threw a hint of truculence into his words. 'It would be walking into the lion's den. I can't do it.'

'Oh, yes, you can,' Smith said. 'And if you don't find what you want there, you'll go on to Mannering's flat. Know where that is?'

Mannering gave a surly shake to his head.

'I'll give you the address,' said Smith. 'No

ducking and no double-crossing, Brown, or I'll have that disguise off you, and that's the way you'll look when the police arrive. Understand?'

'But I can't—'

'What tools have you brought with you?'

'I'll have to go and get them.'

'No you won't. You'll use what we can give you. You'll get your two hundred pounds when you've finished the job—that's if you finish it properly. Otherwise—' Smith turned his thumb downwards. 'Don't make any mistake.'

'I tell you it's crazy!'

'Maybe it is. But you'll do it. When you first came here I didn't know where you lived or anything about you, but I've found out a lot since then.'

'I wish I hadn't had anything to do with you,' whined Mannering. 'I've got along allright by myself—'

'You'll get your orders from Mick,' Smith said sharply. 'He'll tell you where to take the stuff.'

'I don't fancy—'

'You don't have to worry about what you fancy,' Smith said. 'Fix him up with tools, Mick, and then take him round. Keep your eyes on him.'

Menace travelled from man to man.

They did not know that he was Mannering; but they had told him exactly what they were going to do. It wasn't hard to guess. If he found the documents, they would kill him. But the documents wouldn't be found.

Would they use him again?

He might snatch at a chance to-night: work on Mick, if necessary. But first, win Mick's confidence—

* * *

A taxi waited outside, with a man at the wheel. Mick climbed in after Mannering, who carried a waist-band roll of tools, not unlike his own. Mick had told him that in the back of the taxi there was an oxy-acetylene outfit.

They passed Larraby near the Austin.

Larraby would follow; would that be good or bad? Mick would probably notice the Austin.

He was smoking.

Mannering said: 'We can't start yet.'

'You can have a good look at both places, to see the best way of getting in.'

'Sure—sure.'

'And you'd better not make excuses.'

'It's a crazy job,' Mannering muttered.

'You're taking the risk, too, you ought to be more careful.'

'Just you do what you're told.'

'Okay,' Mannering said, and sank back, sulkily.

★   ★   ★

He could so easily deal with Mick, the driver and Smith. He could attract police attention and hand these two men over; take Bristow to the garage and be sure that there was damning evidence there, against all three. It was the easiest thing he had ever been able to do, but—he wouldn't know the whole solution if he did that. He wouldn't know the Shadow; or the final truth. There was personal tragedy here, strong emotional currents which might mar Celia for life; and mar others. He had to go on.

Any lingering possibility that Smith was the Shadow, had gone completely. If Smith were able to break into houses as easily as the thief, he wouldn't have employed 'Brown'. Nor did Smith know other cracksmen on whom he could rely; he wouldn't have used an unknown man, if there had been. Smith was just a receiver, and the Shadow was still unknown.

Smith was cock-a-hoop now. He would probably telephone the flat, for Mannering, just to brag. Smith was so sure that he held the trumps.

They reached Bond Street.

Mick said: 'Here you are—first on the left, it's Hart Row. *Quinns* is the third shop along.'

Mannering got out with a certain show of reluctance. He saw a car coming towards them, and when it passed, recognised the Austin with Larraby at the wheel. Mannering turned towards *Quinns*. The narrow street was empty, and there was only one light. Those at the dress salon next door were fairly bright, but in *Quinns*, the main illumination was at the end of the shop, to enable patrolling police to see that all was well.

Mannering made a pretence of examining the front door, then walked towards the end of the street. Half way along was a narrow alley, which led to the back of *Quinns*. Mannering knew that the only way of forcing entry was by a window or from the roof; both were difficult, and would take time.

He stood looking at the windows.

Sylvester had locked them all; Sylvester would take no chance. The burglar alarm system would be on, but there was no danger from that. Mannering knew exactly where to find it, what measures to take against it. He could convince Mick that he was an artist at his job all right, but—what would happen when he failed to find the documents? What had Smith and Mick planned? Was it murder?

Mick loomed at his elbow.

'Not so much messing about. Just get into that shop.'

'*Now?*' Mannering's voice rose. 'With the police passing every few minutes!'

Mick pressed a gun into his ribs.

'Now,' he said.

     ★   ★   ★

It was remarkable how little he knew about his own premises; the unexpected fittings, the care with which the burglar alarm system had been installed. It wasn't made easier by the presence of Mick, with the gun. There was little risk of them being seen at the back, except by the patrolling police, and Mannering lost no time forcing the window. He crept cautiously along the narrow passages and down the stairs, as if he were feeling his way. He used a hooded torch; and all the time, Mick followed him. He reached the office door. If he worked at it, he would be seen in the light; that was the great risk.

He kept in the shadows.

'Having a nap?' Mick sneered.

'Go and see if the police are around,' Mannering said. 'I'm not going to start here until they've passed on the next round. We'll have half an hour, then.'

Mick crept towards the window. There was absolute silence in the shop. Then someone appeared outside, and a torch shone into the window. The beam was diffused by the glass. With the light fixed near the office door, added to the torch glow, Mannering could see Mick clearly; and he knew that a constable was outside.

The man tried the door, shook it vigorously, and then passed on.

Mick crept back. 'Okay, now.'

The lock was a good one; it would have been much more difficult to open, if Mannering hadn't known the mechanism inside out. As it was, it took ten minutes. When the door opened, Mick stepped swiftly past him. Mick wasn't a fool. He found the safe, almost at once; and found, also that it led to vaults in the cellar. He didn't keep his gun in sight, but gave orders peremptorily. He examined the contents of the safe, and swore when there were none of the papers.

Mannering muttered: 'You make too much noise. How do you expect me to do my job?'

'You just do it,' Mick said.

There were no documents at Quinns; Mick was forced to accept this fact when they had opened the last of the five big safes in the strong room. But there were hundreds of thousands of pounds worth of jewels and *objets d'art*. When he'd finished his fruitless search Mick stood back in speculation.

'We could get away with a fortune, and by gum we will. I saw a couple of suitcases upstairs. Get them.'

Mannering went upstairs, taking longer than was necessary. He found the cases, and together they crammed the jewels and small *objets* into them.

'If Mannering gets on to us,' Mannering began, 'he'll—'

'Don't you worry about that. We'll fix Mannering some other way.' Mick took something from his pocket—a small canister, with a round lid. He put it by a safe, then took it away. 'No, I know a better place.'

'Where is it?'

'Just mind your own business.'

Mannering shrugged, and led the way upstairs. In the office, Mick put the canister in the middle drawer of the desk. He half closed the drawer. Mannering watched him closely.

'I want to know what that is.'

'If you read about a fire in the morning, you'll know,' said Mick. '*If* you read about it!'

The hint of menace was strong; but Mannering almost missed it. The canister obviously contained explosive or liquid fire; it was probably worked mechanically, and would go off during the night. If it were efficient, and Smith probably would make sure of that, it would start a blaze that might demolish Quinns.

He could deal with Mick, now, and remove the fire-canister; or he could wait a little longer.

'Get a move on, we've finished here,' Mick said.

They got out unseen, loaded the cases into the taxi, climbed in, and drove off. Mick didn't speak. Mannering wiped his neck, and watched a policeman on his rounds. They reached Oxford Street, turned into a narrow side street, where another cab was waiting.

'We change cabs here,' Mick said.

'Why'

'You talk too much!'

The cab with the fortune from Quinns moved off. Mick and Mannering sat in the other, and Mick told the driver to make for

Chelsea.

Mannering said: 'We can't do the flat yet, there's bound to be someone there!'

'There won't. Smith's fixed it.'

Mannering said: 'He can't fix Mannering like that!'

'If we come across Mannering, we'll know what to do,' Mick said. 'You just obey orders.'

'His wife—'

Mick laughed. 'Don't you worry about his wife. She had a message a little while ago, and she left in a hurry. She won't come back quite so quickly, though.'

CHAPTER TWENTY-SEVEN

SECOND BURGLARY

Mannering said harshly: 'You take too many chances. You haven't hurt her, have you?'

'What's that to you?'

'Plenty,' Mannering said. 'I don't want to get mixed up in any violence. I've never done a violent job in my life.'

'You'll be in one now, if you don't stop talking,' Mick said.

Mannering sat back in the corner, flaming anxiety in his mind. He didn't question the truth of Mick's statement; he could believe that Lorna, not expecting to be involved, would be easily fooled by a message. Smith had hit back, hard and fast; first Celia, now Lorna. Mannering kept his gaze away from Mick, hardly able to trust himself to keep still.

They were held up in a traffic block.

'What are all these papers about?' he demanded.

'The Boss wants them, that's good enough for you.'

Mannering said: 'Kidnapping's a serious charge.'

'You didn't snatch her, did you?'

'I'm mixed up in it.' He kept the whining note in his voice. 'I won't stand for murder—understand?'

'You won't have to.' Mick gave the little self-satisfied laugh that betrayed a criminal's vanity. 'We've got it all laid on.'

They reached King's Road, and turned into River Walk. Bristow's man did not show up in the doorway opposite; the time he was wanted most—

Forget it.

Mick knew where Lorna was, and the two women were probably together. Smith wasn't likely to keep them in Buckley Street. They might be at the garage—might have been there when he had arrived.

The taxi pulled up at the end of the street.

'Back way,' said Mick. 'I've had a good look round this place, and it's easy. There are some staples in the wall leading to Mannering's window. It's in a dark spot, too, you won't be seen.'

'We ought to try the front door, if it's a flat.'

'Maybe you're right at that,' Mick said, slowly.

They went into the house, unobserved. Lights were on at the downstairs flat, but none on the next floor. He picked the lock of his own door, and for the first time that night, his hands were unsteady. He pushed the door open cautiously, and crept in. Mick followed him, and immediately put on the light.

Mannering hissed: 'Put that off! There might be a servant.'

'She's up in the loft, tied up. Smith didn't like her.' Mick sniggered. 'You're too nervous, that's your trouble.'

'I could do with a drink,' said Mannering hoarsely.

'Not a bad idea.' Mick was unexpectedly affable. 'I'll find where he keeps it, you look for the safe.'

The only safe in the flat was inside an old oak settle, in the study. It had a false seat, and a steel, electrically protected safe inside. It was one of the last places he would be expected to look. He went through the study, tapping the floorboards and the walls, pulling up corners of the carpet. Mike came in with a bottle of Johnnie Walker, a syphon and two glasses. He put them down and rubbed his hands together vigorously.

'Pity to burn this stuff up.'

'You've left another of those things?'

'That's right,' Mick said. 'Mannering's going to be sorry he got in Smith's way.' He poured out two drinks, tossed his own down, and then scowled. 'Haven't you found the safe?'

'Not yet. There may only be the one at Quinns.'

'Don't be a fool. Where've you looked?'

Mannering pointed, and sipped his drink. Mick kicked the end of the settle.

'Well, try this.'

Mannering said: 'It's no use looking there,' but went across.

* * *

There were few jewels in the settle safe; most of his stock was at Quinns. They took out some of Lorna's jewellery, and Mick dropped it into his pocket. He poured himself out another drink, and swore at Mannering—the 'absent' Mannering—for failing to keep the papers here. Then he started to search the flat, ripping out drawers, taking down pictures, looking for another hiding place. Mannering poured him out a third whisky; it seemed to have little more effect on him than water.

'He'll be roaring mad,' Mick said. 'Roaring mad. He was sure we'd find it.'

'I've done *my* best.'

'I'll say that for you.' Mick dropped his hand to his pocket, and Mannering knew that it was closing about his gun. 'I'd better give him a ring.'

Mannering didn't protest.

Mick dialled; Mannering refilled his glass, and the man hardly seemed to notice. He stood with the receiver at his ear for a long time. At last he said: 'We're at the flat. They're not here.'

Mannering muttered: 'I'll go over the other room again.' He went out, slipping into the bedroom; there was an extension telephone on the bedside table. He picked it up, and heard Smith's voice. It was damning Mick, 'Brown' and everyone who failed to do his job properly. He sounded at a high pitch of nervous tension.

'Brown still with you?'

'Sure. You said I wasn't to finish him until I'd found the books. He's good, I'll say that for him, never seen anyone pick a lock like he can. We might find him useful.'

'Those things must be at the flat or Quinns.'

'But they're not!'

There was a pause; then Smith said: 'Did you leave the tins?'

'Sure. And I want to be away before two

o'clock.'

'You'd better come here,' Smith said. 'What else did you pick up?'

'Plenty, especially from Q.'

'It will be a help,' Smith said. 'We'll have to clear out. I've got the tickets, we can leave tonight. Mannering won't do anything while we've got his wife, we'll have time. You haven't run into him, have you?'

'No, neither place.'

'He's probably with Fleming,' Smith said. 'I'll talk to him. You come straight here.'

'With Brown?'

Smith swore at him.

'Okay, okay, I'll leave him to roast,' Mick said.

He put down the telephone. So did Mannering. Mick called out: 'Where the hell are you?' and came out of the study. He saw the light on in the bedroom. 'What are you wasting time in here for?'

Mannering said: 'I think I've found something.'

'*What?*' Mick came almost excitedly into the room, his right hand snatched from his pocket. Mannering was behind the door, on one knee, reaching under the bed. Mick bent down and lifted the bedspread, and Mannering straightening up, caught the man under the chin with the back of his head. Mick's teeth snapped together and he jolted back. Mannering thrust his hand swiftly into his pocket, and whipped out the gun. He was covering Mick as the man fell against the bed, so shocked by this development that he almost forgot the pain.

Mannering said: 'So you was going to kill me.' Mick put up his hands, as if to fend him off. 'Well, you've got another think coming. So has Smith. Where *is* Smith?'

'Put—put that gun down!'

Mannering raised the gun, covering Mick's face. The man had drunk too much whisky, and the effect was beginning to show. His hands shook, his legs were unsteady.

'Tell me where Smith is, or I'll blow your brains out.'

'Get away!' screeched Mick. 'Get away! He's at Leven Street, Victoria, 9 Leven Street. *Get away!*'

'You got a key?'

'No! No, he wouldn't let me have one.' Mick gasped despairingly, seeing Mannering loom over him. '*Get away*. I haven't got a key. I have to go to the back door, there's a bell under the knocker, a special bell. *Get away!*'

Mannering's fist crashed into his chin. As he slumped over the bed, Mannering hit him on the right temple with the butt of his gun, then picking him up bodily, carried him into the kitchen. He bound his wrists and ankles with cord from a drawer, forcing himself to do everything carefully; if he lost his head he would lose valuable time. He pushed Mick into the larder and locked the door on him, then went into the drawing-room. He stood looking round; nothing seemed to be disturbed. He went across to the piano; the canister wasn't there. He found it beneath the writing desk near the window, and dropped it into his pocket.

He hadn't much time.

He went into the bedroom, and began wiping the greasepaint off his face. 'Brown' faded into the past. He had to be thorough. He rubbed his face with spirit and examined it carefully. Changing quickly into one of his own suits, be put the canister into one pocket, Mick's gun in another, then bundled the clothes up into a parcel, which he tied with string.

Then he went upstairs.

Hetty, bound and gagged, lay in a corner, unconscious. He cut the cords, and took the gag away, and left her. Downstairs, he put the bundle over his shoulder and went to the door.

Before he reached it, he heard someone approaching.

Bristow?

He dropped the bundle behind a hall chair, and the canister on top of it. The front door bell rang. He lit a cigarette before he opened the door, fully expecting to see Bristow.

Fleming stood there.

CHAPTER TWENTY-EIGHT

THE SHADOW

'Hallo, Mannering.' Fleming came in briskly. 'I'm glad I've caught you. Do you know that Smith has taken Celia back?'

'Yes,' said Mannering. 'She isn't alone. My wife's with her.'

Fleming said: 'Your wife!' He looked dumbfounded. 'Do you mean to say that—'

'He's played himself into my hands, and this is his way of getting out again,' Mannering said. 'I think he's planning a getaway, and he'll probably take Celia with him. He won't want to be handicapped with my wife.' The words sounded as bleak as he felt. 'I'm going to his place, now. I shall leave a message for the police to raid it soon afterwards. Final showdown with Mr. Smith! If you want to come with me, meet me at Victoria Station in half an hour.'

Mannering waved him away, then locked the door and returned to the kitchen. There was no sound from Mick. He opened the window and climbed out, with the bundle slung over his shoulder. Only a few lighted windows broke the darkness. He hurried to the middle of the patch of waste land near the houses, and placed the bundle, with the canister in the middle, where it could do little harm. Then he made for the main road. He saw the Austin parked at the corner, and Larraby standing in shadows, watching the taxi which was drawn up outside Mannering's front door.

Mannering whispered: 'Josh.'

Larraby started, and turned.

'Josh, listen to me.' Mannering rested his hand on the smaller man's shoulder. 'I've an urgent job. Mrs. Mannering is with Smith. Never mind the details. They're at 9 Leven Street, Victoria. I want half an hour's grace, then telephone Bristow.'

'Very good, sir.' Larraby's soft voice was itself a reassurance.

'When you've done that, go to your hotel and collect the parcel of books and papers which you'll find addressed to you. Take it to the Palling garage and leave it there, preferably in Smith's room. I don't think you'll find anyone at the garage. If you do, drop the stuff and then call the police. After that, go to the shop. There's a tin in the middle drawer of the office desk—highly inflammable. Get rid of it. All clear?'

'Perfectly.'

'Is there anything else to report?' Mannering asked.

'A man just called at your house, sir, driving a Humber.'

'Fleming, that's all right. Get another car, I need this one.'

Larraby nodded. Mannering climbed into the Austin and turned towards Victoria. He reached the station in ten minutes, pulled up outside it, and went to look for Fleming. There was no sign of the man. He waited for five minutes, and then inquired of a taxi-driver, for Leven Street. It was nearby, and Number 9 was one of a terrace of tall narrow houses, served by a service alley. It was in one of the backwaters of London, a Georgian house with an iron balcony and a fine wrought iron gate.

He went round to the back.

As he reached the gateway leading to a small, narrow garden, he thought he heard a sound, as of a door opening. He stood quite still, then tried the handle of the gate and it moved at a touch. He looked through, and saw the faint shadow of a man disappearing into the house. Mannering gave him a few seconds to get through the room, then tried the handle of the door. It had been forced swiftly and expertly.

Mannering opened it just wide enough to get through. He saw the final shadow of a man's figure advancing along a narrow passage. The door of this room, a kitchen, was ajar, and the light came from the front hall.

The man reached the foot of a flight of stairs, and when he turned, the light fell on his face. Mannering, pressed tightly against the wall, his presence unsuspected, recognised Fleming.

* * *

Fleming had forced the lock of the gate and of the back door. Both locks would defeat any but a first-class cracksman.

Was *Fleming* the Shadow?

* * *

Mannering kept close to the staircase, as Fleming went up. There was no sound in the house. Mannering stayed by the wall, straining his ears. Fleming moved silent as a wraith. There was a long, tense pause. A car travelled along the street, its engine sounding loud; but when it faded, there was a silence so full that Mannering could hear his own breathing and the beating of his heart.

Then upstairs a door crashed back.

Fleming said: 'Don't move!'

Mannering reached the end of the passage. The light was brighter now, coming from a room on the landing. There was no sound of any answering voice. Mannering crept stealthily up the stairs. Half-way up, he could see Fleming standing in a doorway with his back towards him. He could see, also, the gun in Fleming's hand. He couldn't see Smith.

There was a squat cupboard on the landing. Mannering quickened his pace. He caught a glimpse of Smith's face, set in a stare of frigid surprise as it glared at Fleming.

Mannering reached the cover of the cupboard. He could see part of Fleming's back and a corner of the room; and could hear everything, even the long, slow intake of breath as Smith began to speak.

'So Major Fleming has finally come out in his true colours!'

'Move back,' Fleming said.

'Major Fleming *alias* the Shadow. You haven't forgotten that little fact, have you? You haven't forgotten that I've proof against you which will be handed to the police whether I live or die?'

'Move back,' Fleming said. Smith apparently obeyed, for Fleming edged forward. 'I have forgotten nothing.'

'Nothing except a few little things which seem to have slipped an accommodating memory. Put that gun away, Shadow. It won't help you.'

'It'll help,' Fleming said. 'I'm still a good shot, and before I leave here you'll be a dead man. You've had it coming for a long time, Smith. You've blackmailed me for six years, and it's all over.'

'Of course I've blackmailed you. You were a sitting pigeon. An ex-Army officer with a distinguished record *couldn't* allow it to be suspected that he was a cracksman, could he? In plainer words, a thief. I advise you to drop that gun, Fleming.'

'Keep where you are,' Fleming answered. His voice was steady. 'You've had a long run. You started turning the screw on my wife. I had to give way. I couldn't satisfy you, and I turned to burglary. You discovered it. You had me where you wanted me, and made Celia's life a hell. But then you went too far.'

'Hanging's an ugly death,' Smith said.

'I shan't hang. I shall shoot myself. First you, then myself—after I've released Mannering's wife and Celia. Mannering will look after Celia, and do a better job than I'll be able to do.'

'You're crazy!' The first edgy note was discernible in Smith's voice.

'You think I'm crazy. Smith, I've done all this for one reason: to help my wife. You wouldn't understand it, but I loved her. I built my life around her. You fastened on to her weakness, deliberately, and for your own foul purpose, then telephoned her, to say that Muriel was coming. She's told me that. You lied to her, saying that Muriel was my mistress. Remember? You wanted Muriel dead and my wife and I hanged for it. It nearly worked; she killed Muriel. I discovered it and covered her tracks. But the shock was too great. My wife died this evening.'

Smith caught his breath.

'You killed her as surely, as relentlessly, as if you'd cut her throat,' said Fleming. 'You've made her last years hell. Yet your life was on sufferance, because I daren't risk killing you, daren't risk the truth coming out—she needed me so much. She doesn't need me any more. Now do you understand why I've come?'

Smith didn't speak.

Fleming said: 'Where is Celia? Where is Mrs. Mannering?'

'You—won't find out!' The words came in a rush.

'I'll find out,' said Fleming, 'but you can make it easier for me. And for yourself. If you tell me, I'll shoot you in the head. If you don't, I'll shoot you in the stomach, where it will hurt. Understand—*hurt.*' Fleming's voice was so quiet that the words hardly seemed to hold their true meaning. 'Where are they?'

'Fleming, put that gun away! Talk sense! I've a fortune here—I made a big haul tonight. I emptied Mannering's shop of everything that could be brought away. I've a fortune salted away in several countries; we needn't keep up this vendetta. Put the gun away and talk business.'

'Where are they?' asked Fleming. 'I haven't much time. Mannering's coming, with the police, I don't want any interruption. Where are the women?'

'*Put that gun away!*'

'I shall give you ten seconds,' Fleming said.

There was silence; but a clock was ticking. Fleming raised his arm, Mannering could just see the movement. He wished he could see Smith's face.

Smith muttered: 'They're here, upstairs. They're all right! Fleming, I've finished with Celia, you needn't worry about that any more. You can't blame me because she fell in love with me, that was her fault, it wasn't mine. She's not quite sane, you know that. She's like her mother, she—'

'Keep your foul mouth shut!'

Smith cried: 'Don't shoot, don't—'

Mannering moved from his hiding place, swept an arm round, and struck Fleming on the shoulder. A shot roared out. Mannering saw Smith, half-turning, hands in front of his face trying to get away. The bullet missed. Fleming swung round on Mannering, and Mannering gripped his right wrist, twisted and forced the gun out of his grasp.'

'Get the women,' Mannering snapped. 'Don't worry about Smith.' He thrust Fleming aside and went into the room, as Smith dropped his right hand to his pocket. Mannering flicked the gun from his hand.

Smith said unevenly, his face ashen: 'Mannering, I'll give you a fortune if you'll let me go.'

'My own fortune?' Mannering asked politely.

'You can have that back, *and* fifty thousand pounds in addition. I've got to get away before the police arrive. I've got everything ready, passport, passage—everything. I won't come back, I won't worry Celia again, you needn't worry. Let me go, let me get away.'

Mannering said. 'Where's the evidence against the Shadow?'

'It—' Smith broke off. 'Mannering, if I tell you, will you let me go?'

'It's your only chance. Where's the evidence?'

'If I tell you—'

'*Where is it?*'

'It's in the safe at the garage, you missed that. It's all there, you can have the triumph of your life *and* be able to laugh at the police from now to Doomsday. Mannering—' the man's thin lips were working, his eyes had a frenzied look. 'Let me go, the money's here, I've turned everything I could lay my hands on into cash to-day. I knew I'd have to get away. Your wife's all right.' He eased his collar. 'I wasn't going to hurt her, I was only fooling, she's not hurt. Celia isn't either, she—'

There was a sound behind Mannering. He didn't turn round.

Lorna said: 'John—'

He kept looking at Smith.

'Are you all right?'

'Yes,' Lorna said, her voice low. 'Celia's here.'

'Get her away. Take her to the flat. Look after Hetty, she's up in the studio, and send for the police, there's a man locked in the larder. Say you found him and that I know nothing about it. I'll be there soon.' He watched Smith lynx-eyed. 'Where's Fleming?'

'Here,' Fleming said.

'Look in the safe at Palling Garage, Palling Street,' Mannering said. 'You'll find some of the contents interesting. Then come to my flat. Send for George Lee, and we'll have a party.'

Smith screeched: 'Mannering, you've got everything you want, you can catch the Shadow. You can—'

'Hurry,' Mannering said.

'We're on our way,' said Fleming. There were footsteps and muted voices. The front door opened, and closed sharply; and silence fell.

Smith broke it.

'Mannering, you can take everything that's here, you will be worth a fortune. Just give me an hour's start of the police, that's all I want.'

Mannering said: 'You're not much of an ornament to society, Smith. You aren't much good to yourself or to anyone else. There isn't a chance of escape. I caught Mick and another man at my flat. The other man escaped. Mick didn't. Mick will confess. You'll get a long stretch—ten or fifteen years. They might even get you for murder.'

There was sweat on Smith's forehead, his face was like a death's head.

'Let me go, give me a start, I won't harm anyone else.'

Mannering said:

'I wouldn't trust you for five seconds. You'll be arrested to-night, charged, go to the Magistrate's Court in the morning and be remanded for eight days. Then there'll be a fuller hearing. After that, you'll be committed for trial. You'll have the full glare of publicity. You'll stand in the dock, knowing you won't have a chance. Ten years in jail, at least, the whole story told—'

'I couldn't stand it!'

Mannering tossed the gun on to a chair.

'The police will be here in a few minutes,' he said, and went out and closed the door. He turned the key in the lock and waited.

He had been there, in the semi-darkness, for several minutes, when he heard a car draw up outside; this would be Bristow. He stared at the locked door. There was a harsh ringing of the front door bell.

From the room, a shot rang out.

★ ★ ★

Bristow was at the head of the three men who ran up the stairs. Mannering stood waiting for them. Bristow said abruptly: 'Was that a shot?'

'It wouldn't surprise me.'

'Who was it?'

'Probably the Shadow. You know him as Smith.'

Bristow looked at the door, and said sharply: 'The key's on the outside.'

'I locked him in.'

Bristow grunted, and thrust the door open. Smith was lying on his side, with his back to the door. His right hand was stretched out, and the gun lay within an inch of it. Bristow moved across and Mannering and the others followed.

Smith *moved*.

He grabbed the gun, twisted round, and pointed it at Mannering; and there was hatred in his eyes, the old glitter, as if the Devil were back in the man. Mannering hadn't time to move, saw the trigger finger squeeze—and then his legs were hooked from under him by one of Bristow's men, and he crashed down. He felt the bullet bite into his left arm. He didn't see Bristow jump at Smith or see Smith put the gun to his mouth and fire again.

CHAPTER TWENTY-NINE

SHADOW LIFTED

With his arm in a sling, Mannering walked up the stairs to his Chelsea flat. He didn't have to use his key, for the door opened and Lorna appeared. She stretched out one hand and took his, and he put his arm round her shoulders. As they moved into the hall, Hetty appeared.

Mannering smiled at her. 'I'm terribly sorry that you had such a scare.'

'*Scare!* I was terrified! If that man ever comes here again, I'll leave, I couldn't stand—'

'He won't come again,' Mannering said. 'He's dead. Make some coffee, will you?'

'Dead!' echoed Hetty.

She was still standing there, undecided which mood would yield the best dramatic effect, when, arm in arm with Lorna, he moved into the drawing-room. Celia, her back to the window, turned and stared at him. There was no doubt, from her expression, that she had heard what had been said.

There was shock there, horror, and perhaps relief.

Mannering poured out a whisky and soda, and took it across to her. She sipped a little, and then put the glass down, as if she must know the truth.

'How did it happen?'

'He killed himself,' Mannering said. 'He also killed your mother, Celia.'

'*Killed* her!'

'The shock was too much for her, and she died tonight.' Whisky was spilling over her glass and dripping to the carpet. 'He gave her too much to drink, egged her on to kill Muriel, and wanted your father hanged for it. When he knew that he would have to stand trial, he shot himself. It was over very quickly.'

She steadied the glass, and drank again.

'He was planning to leave the country without you,' Mannering said.

She nodded, as if she understood the full significance of that.

'And listen, Celia,' Mannering said quietly. 'I don't know what he did to set you against your father, but whatever it was, was false. Your father sacrificed everything he had, to save your mother, and paid him a fortune in blackmail. Remember that.'

Celia said unsteadily: 'Paul told me—' she looked round as if for help, but no help was there.

'He told me that it was not my mother who had killed that woman in South Africa, but my father. I hated him for putting the blame on her. Was—wasn't it true?'

'No,' said Mannering. 'Your mother wasn't quite normal, Celia, and your father protected her in every way he could.'

Celia turned to Lorna, and together they moved to a chair. She was still sitting there when Larraby arrived, twenty minutes later. The canister, he reported, was at the bottom of the Thames.

He was in the kitchen, with Hetty, when the telephone bell rang. Mannering answered it.

'Mannering speaking.'

'Put me through to Mr. Brown, please,' a man said crisply.

Mannering exclaimed: '*Brown!* There's no one named Brown here.'

'He must have moved,' said Bristow, airily. 'One day he may not move fast enough.'

Before Mannering could reply, he rang off.

Fleming and Lee were coming in, Lee with exuberant excitement.

* * *

Mannering said: 'Did you find those

papers?'

'I've burnt them,' said Fleming.

'Burnt what?' asked Lee.

'Forget it,' Mannering said. 'Celia's in the other room. She knows everything, and took the shock better than I thought she would. She'll probably be all right after a few weeks rest. Don't force anything on her. If my wife and I can help, we will. I'd say the best thing would be for her to have a holiday in a country cottage, with some friends of mine. She'll be all right.'

'She *must* be!' cried Lee.

'She will be,' Fleming said, and he smiled, as if at some happy memory.

* * *

Celia was sleeping in the spare room, Fleming and Lee had gone, and Mannering and Lorna were sitting in the drawing-room, when the front door bell rang. Lorna, who regarded Mannering's wounded arm as if it were a major injury, jumped up to open the door.

Chittering, with a plaster over his forehead and a bruise on his chin, came in briskly. The bruise distorted his smile, but his eyes were glowing.

'Hallo, John. I'm told you've been in the wars.'

'Just a skirmish.'

'And that you handed a dead Shadow to Bristow on a plate.'

'Nice of him to say so.'

'He didn't mince words. He's been to this garage which Smith ran under the name of Caton, and found all the proof he needed. As well as most of the proceeds of the Shadow's recent hauls. Insurance companies owe you a nice fat cheque! I gather that Celia's not hurt.'

'She's here, sleeping.'

'Trust the Mannerings,' Chittering said, and sat down. 'Mind if I rest? No, thanks, I won't have whisky, I'm told that it would give me a whacking great headache. Mind telling me the inside story?'

Mannering laughed. 'You know it.'

'Not one half,' Chittering said. 'But I suppose I can't expect any more from you. I've a splash headline, and your picture will be on the front page. I'm told that one of the Shadow's men fell foul of you—trying to burgle the place.'

'Something like that.'

'He babbled on about a man called Brown. Bristow is very interested in this Mr. Brown.

Any idea who he is?'

'Not a notion,' said Mannering.

'Strange! That reminds me, there's a big bonfire outside, they've had to call the fire brigade out. I wonder what started that off.'

'Mischievous boys, probably,' Mannering said.

★ ★ ★

Six months later, when the trial of Mick and the other men was over, the Mannerings received an invitation to spend a weekend at Guildford. They reached Maylands early in the afternoon, and found Fleming in the orchard, and George Lee cleaning carburettors, in the garage. Lee called: 'I'll be with you in a jiffy.' Fleming came hurrying, and opened the front gate.

'How's business?' asked Mannering.

'Flourishing,' said Fleming, and laughed. 'I'm much happier in my new job!'

'Past really is the past?'

'I saw enough of hell not to want to go back,' Fleming said. 'No one suspects the truth, and Celia—' he gripped Mannering's arm tightly. 'She's full recovered. I think she and George will marry. He's found a useful job, and is doing quite well.'

'I'm so glad,' Lorna said.

'Mannering, why did you give me that chance?' Fleming asked. 'I've never worked that out. There seemed no reason why—'

'Let's say I'd seen a glimpse of the same hell,' said Mannering lightly. 'Hallo, there she is.'

Her dark hair blowing back, her eyes bright, with contentment, Celia hurried towards them.

'Was it worth it?' Mannering asked.

Lorna laughed.

CANCELLED AND SOLD BY
FRIENDS OF THE
EUCLID PUBLIC LIBRARY
FOR
THE BENEFIT OF THE LIBRARY

A000603279761
0000603279761
061002
MYSTERY   BGL-3824
24
Creasey, John.
Shadow the baron

S92/4
J93/4
C94
T95/1

EUCLID PUBLIC LIBRARY
631 EAST 222nd STREET
EUCLID, OHIO 44123
216-261-5300

EXTENSION SERVICE

DEMCO